I0727132

WAHIDA CLARK PRESENTS

THOT

"She always gets what she wants!"

A NOVEL BY

ALAH ADAMS

T.H.O.T!
That Ho Out There

BY ALAH ADAMS

Wahida Clark Presents Publishing, LLC
60 Evergreen Place
Suite 904
East Orange, New Jersey 07018
973-678-9982
www.wclarkpublishing.com

ISBN 13-digit 978-1-936649-25-9
ISBN 10-digit 193664925X
eBook ISBN 9781936649068

Library of Congress Catalog Number
1. Urban, Suspense, Drugs, Hustle, New York City, African-American, Street Lit – Fiction

Cover design and layout by Nuance Art, LLC
Book interior design by www.aCreativeNuance.com
Contributing Editors: Linda Wilson and R. Hamilton

Printed in United States

SPECIAL THANKS

I want to give thanks and praise to the Creative Forces of the Universe for blessing me with the talented gift of writing. This has been the most meaningful experience of my life. I am in Love with writing and I will continue to write until the candle is blown out! This time around I have different types of people I want to thank, people that don't even know I exist.

The biggest thanks goes out to Mrs. Shonda Rhimes Of SHONDALAND. I studied all of her shows to develop a better writing style for myself. Thot is the first novel I wrote with sub-titles in the chapters. I wanted all the chapters to flow like an episode of SCANDAL or HOW TO GET AWAY WITH MURDER. So I look forward to my fans critiquing my new style. Hopefully you'll enjoy it as much as I enjoyed experimenting with a different style. If anyone knows Shonda, tell her Alah Adams would love to write for her if she'll have me on board.

It's funny because I started writing Thot 2 years ago when the word was still fresh. Please excuse the wait, but you'll see that it was well worth it. I want to thank the Usual Suspects, the mainstays in my life. These people inspire me by virtue of just living, my four children; Alah Jr., Dejour, Elijah and Princess Audrey. I have a new edition to my family since the last release. My grandson

Princeton, Papa loves you.   Last but not least, I want to thank my beautiful Queen Lisa for patience and Love.

This book is dedicated to the memory of Stephanie 'Fefa' Rivera and the one and only true Prince Rogers Nelson.

PROLOGUE

Vinny hid in the bedroom closet of the plush condo he purchased for Chasity. Heart racing with anxiety, he opened the bottle of Oxycodone he held and popped two pills. He shed tears as he listened to Torian pounding her vagina as if he were killing her.

"Oh my god!" Chasity screamed out in ecstasy. "You are the best! Keep fucking me!"

Furious, Vinny's chest heaved, and he couldn't control his jaw from grinding. His hand shook, almost causing him to drop his weapon and the pills. He shoved the bottle back into his pants pocket. *I can't believe this is happening. I trusted her with everything, and this is how she repays me.* Vinny cocked the .45 caliber ACP pistol. *I knew I should've listened to Rocco.* He sniffled. The effects of the powerful opiate was starting to kick in.

"What's that noise?" Torian asked, stopping mid-stroke after hearing a clicking of some kind. "Sounds like somebody's in the closet." Torian dismounted Chasity and grabbed his pants where he'd concealed his 9-millimeter. Before he could grip his weapon, Vinny rushed out of the closet busting shots.

Bang! Bang! Bang!

The first shot hit Torian in his shoulder, pushing him two steps back. He fell to the floor about two feet from his 9-millimeter. He lay there not making a sound, pretending to be unconscious, yet inching his hand toward his gun. The other two bullets landed in the headboard right by Chasity's head.

"Vinny!" she screamed and flinched, holding her arms up in the air. "Baby, please put the gun down . . . It's not what it looks like."

"That's all you have to say!" He looked at her with red teary eyes, seething in anger.

Bang!

He let off a shot right by her head. Tears streamed down Vinny's face. "I gave you *everything!* I took you from living in motels selling your ass, to a condo and a BMW! And this is how you repay me!" He lunged toward her as if to strike her with the butt of his gun.

She quickly guarded her head with her hands. "Wait! I can explain!" She forced a smile in an attempt to calm him down.

"I don't want to hear it!" Vinny pointed the gun at Chasity. "I should kill you!"

Torian got his hand on his gun, but he didn't have a clear shot at Vinny because of the angle. Vinny moved closer to Chasity, putting the gun to her head, which gave Torian the perfect advantage. Just as Torian's index finger pressed on the trigger, Vinny saw him in his peripheral, turned, and let off two shots in rapid succession.

Bang! Bang!

One of the shots hit Torian in his chest, but not before Torian let off three shots at the same time. Two shots hit Vinny in his neck; the third shot pierced the closet door. He slumped to the ground while gurgling on his blood. Both men lay on the floor, gravely injured.

Chasity stood viewing the carnage. Vinny tried to use his hands to squeeze the wounds in his neck to stop the blood from flowing. It was too late; in three minutes his hands unclasped his neck, and he lay peacefully still. Vinny was dead.

She slowly turned to look at Torian as he lay motionless with his eyes wide open staring right at Chasity. Instantly she turned her head and squeezed her eyelids as tight as she could. She opened them and turned back to the same horrific scene. The man she really loved was gone.

"This isn't real," she told herself. "Snap out of it!" She couldn't believe what had just happened.

At that moment, her mind had been stripped of its ability to reason. Disoriented, she gazed at both bodies as if they were illusions. Suffolk County police officers entering the room with their guns drawn, brought her out of her trance.

"Get on the floor with your hands behind your head!" the officer yelled.

Unresponsive, Chasity stood there stark naked.

The officer, seeing her blank expression, realized she posed no immediate threat. Cautious, he moved toward her, took one of the blankets that lay on the king-sized bed and covered Chasity's body. The other officers looked at the two bodies on the floor. They glimpsed the .45 caliber ACP next to Vinny, and the 9-millimeter lying next to Torian.

The first officer put his gun away and grabbed Chasity by her shoulders. "Miss, are you all right?"

She remained upright but in a catatonic-like state, experiencing the effects of extreme shock.

After a half hour, the officer took her to a police vehicle, while the homicide squad combed over the scene. It was cut and dry: two men shot each other to death over a woman. It didn't take long for them to surmise the situation.

Still in shock, but no longer catatonic, Chasity was escorted to the precinct where she was placed in a small interrogation room. The officer helped her put clothes on before they left. Now she sat in the cold, gray room looking confused. The door suddenly opened, and in walked a tall, heavyset female with a detective badge hanging from her neck. Her black pantsuit and white button-down shirt fit her frame well.

"How are you doing? My name is Detective Jennifer Colon." She wore a serious expression as she glanced at the paperwork she held. "Miss Chasity Tommyson, that's you, right?"

Chasity met the detective's gaze for a moment before turning her head and looking at the wall. She took a few seconds before speaking. "Yes, that's me."

"Okay, Chasity. Can you tell me what happened today?" Detective Colon slammed the door and looked down at Chasity with disgust. Her long, dark hair fell over her face, hiding her curled lip and heated gaze. She moved her hair aside and stared at Chasity with unfriendly dark brown eyes before taking a seat.

Chasity's eyes widened, but they didn't blink. She seemed to be regressing into her guilty conscience.

"Take your time, take a deep breath," Detective Colon suggested. "If you want me to help you, I need you to tell me how this happened . . . from the beginning."

Slowly, Chasity took in a deep breath and let it out just as measured.

"It all started a year ago when I first met Vinny . . ."

Detective Colon pressed record on the mini video recorder that sat on a tripod. "Okay, take your time. Start from the beginning."

Chasity closed her eyes, but when she opened them she began speaking. "I'm not at all what I appear to be. I have deceived many men by using my looks and my body to lure them into my world of lust. The warning signs were all around me, telling me to stop, telling me that there was danger ahead. But I didn't listen, and now two men are dead. And it's all because of me."

Chasity paused and gazed into the camera wearing a slight smile.

CHAPTER 1

A Sucker, With a Capital 'S!'

Bay Shore Motor Inn
Bay Shore Long Island, New York

Chasity

"Middle fingers up / throw them hands high / middle fingers up/tell em boy bye/boy bye/I aint thinking bout you/Sorry/naw I aint sorry." Chasity sang along with Beyonce to her new single 'Sorry' as it blasted on the radio.

"This is my new anthem! Because I really don't give a fuck about these niggas!" Chasity spoke with passion while she inhaled a huge blunt, then she passed it to Kat.

"My sentiments exactly!" Kat replied as she reached for the blunt and inhaled.

Scantily clad in red Victoria's Secret matching bra and panties, Chasity sat on the bed with her laptop open, checking her traps on the infamous "Front Page" website. Front Page was a way for tricks and 'hos to link up via the Internet. She liked to use the word *trap* to describe the way she enticed weak men into her web of deceit and pleasure.

Chasity was a modern day call girl, a prostitute, otherwise known in the hood as a THOT, an acronym for 'That Ho Out There.'

"The day just started, and I already have three new traps lined up. At $250 apiece, that's $750 for about an hour's worth of work," Chasity said to Kat, her best friend and partner in crime.

"The way these tricks be coming so fast, you can cut that hour into thirty minutes worth of work." Kat inhaled the blunt and then passed it to Chasity.

"I got this one trick that fucks me for the whole hour! I think that nigga be on something before he comes here," Chasity responded.

The days of 'hos walking the strip trying to catch a date were a thing of the past. Nowadays these young thots knew how to use the Internet to their advantage by posting provocative pictures with an implied message. The tricks were up on the new technology, so they went on the sites looking for new 'hos to trick on. That cut out the pimp and the risk of being seen by detectives walking on the 'Thot Trot,' the blocks where primitive thots walked trying to catch a trap.

Chasity and Kat were two of the best 'thots' in Long Island. Both women were voluptuous with gorgeous faces. They were divas, so they always adorned their heads with expensive wigs, kept their toes and nails done, and wore the newest designer labels. They were known to frequent the VIP section in the hottest clubs, buying their own bottles, balling out!

Tall with big brown eyes, Chasity inherited a honey-brown complexion from her Puerto Rican mother and black father. Her pearly white teeth were esthetically pleasing to the eye. When she got dressed up, people often told her she resembled Beyoncé. She kept her stomach flat which made her firm, size 38D cups stand at attention. Chasity was a complete ten!

Kat was a bit shorter, but her ass wasn't. Ass for days, flat stomach, and a nice amount of tits, she was a little darker than Chasity, but people always mistook them for sisters. Chasity and Kat didn't see the resemblance, but they chalked it up to them being around each other so much that they started looking alike. As a team, they were like the dynamic duo.

"That's my number one trap texting me," Kat said when her phone went off. "He's here. I'm going to my room to take care of him."

"Okay, my trap should be here shortly. I'll see you for lunch," Chasity said.

"That sounds like a plan."

Kat went two rooms down. They always got rooms close to each other for safety. Being that they didn't have pimps to protect them, they both kept revolvers close to them at all times. In the past, they had been violated by tricks who knew they didn't have pimps.

Shortly after Kat left the room, Chasity's new trap knocked on the door. She knew it was him, so she sprayed herself with Chanel No. 5 before answering. Her motto was "Go above and beyond to please" to ensure that her traps stayed loyal. She answered the door in her Victoria's Secret undergarments.

"Hi. Vinny, right?" she asked, showing her perfect rows of white teeth.

"Yes, I'm Vinny. You're Cherry?" he asked in a nervous tone. *Wow! This chick is fucking beautiful! I hit the jackpot!* Vinny was stuck in thought standing in the doorway.

She quickly glanced at him from head to toe before inviting him in. "You can come in and make yourself comfortable."

Short, fat, and Italian with slick, black hair, Vinny wasn't quite the looker, but he was very charming. He possessed a gentleman-like quality that made him attractive to women. He was like a knight in shining armor, without the shining armor.

Chasity had a sixth sense for men who were enamored by her. Her 'sucker for love' meter dinged off the charts with this new guy. At first sight she could tell he was smitten by her beauty. She was a pro at tempting men, so she knew exactly how to handle him.

"So, Vinny, what do you do for a living?" she batted her light brown eyes.

"I'm in the construction business." Vinny stared at her in awe.

"Oh, I see . . . construction. Are you a foreman?" she asked.

"No. I own a construction business with my family." Vinny kept rubbing his hands together in an attempt to calm his nerves. *Get it together, Vin!* he thought.

"It must be nice to work with your family."

"Not all the time, but it beats working for some Joe Schmo."

Chasity stared in his eyes and he got weak. She moved closer and he almost jumped. Normally, she would ask for money up front, but she was playing him all the way to the bank. She smelled money like a shark smells plasma.

"Relax, I'm not going to bite you. Unless you tell me to." She smiled, and Vinny seemed to unwind a bit.

Getting right down to business, Chasity unbuckled his belt and pants and pulled his penis out. Vinny almost freaked out, breathing heavily. Immediately, she took him into her mouth as if her life depended on it. The force with which she sucked his penis made Vinny's toes curl in seconds. She felt his sperm swelling up in his balls early, so she slurped with more ferociousness.

"Oh my God!" Vinny yelled out in ecstasy. "I'm coming!"

"Mmmmm! It tastes so good!" Chasity said as she lapped up his semen.

Vinny's eyes rolled around in his head. "You're the best! I mean that."

"Never had any complaints."

"No, really. No woman has ever made me come that fast from sucking my dick before." Vinny took out five 100 dollar bills. "I know you said it was only $250, but you were so good I'm giving you double!"

I got him! Hook, line, and sucker! "Aww, you don't have to do that. You're so sweet, Vinny."

"No, I want you to take it. I want to see you every day if that's possible?" He panted as sweat beads dotted his forehead and nose, looking at her like a puppy that needed attention from its master.

"Of course you can, silly!" Chasity laughed. "You're so funny!"

". . . Can we just cuddle for a minute?" Vinny knew that was a weird question.

"Sure, baby. Take your clothes off and get under the covers. You still have about fifty minutes left."

Vinny did as he was told. He curled up and went to sleep with Chasity as if she were his wife. He was officially open.

Damn this nigga hooked already, and I didn't even throw this tight, wet pussy on him yet. Chasity let him sleep for an hour, then she woke him.

"Wake up, sleepy head. Time to go."

"Damn, I was out of it." Vinny got up and put his clothes on. "So, I'll see you tomorrow at the same time?"

"If that's what you want, honey. I'll be here waiting for you, baby." She kissed him on the cheek.

Vinny finally left, and she watched him walk away to see what model car he drove. When he sat comfortably in a new jet black BMW 650i convertible, she knew she'd hit the jackpot. *Everything about Vinny screams money. And I want it all!*

Just as Vinny was leaving, Chasity got a text from her next client: *I'm pulling in right now.*

Chasity: *Okay, I'm ready.*

She went to the bathroom and rinsed her mouth out with mouthwash and brushed her teeth. As she was finishing up, there was a knock on the door.

With the same smile as before, she answered it. "Hi, Tommy. Come in and make yourself comfortable."

Tommy was a regular, and he wasn't a two-minute man. He was smart enough to pop a Viagra before his weekly appointments. Also, Tommy wasn't rich. He was just a truck driver with an appetite for young thots. Every week he would spend his hard earned money on one hour of pleasure.

Tall and light-skinned, the older black man had been married twice and divorced twice. Although he came equipped with a ten-inch penis, his last girlfriend cheated on him with his best friend, and that's when he decided to deal with women like Chasity and call it a day. For him it was less headaches and no commitment, that's what he enjoyed most about the situation.

Tommy didn't waste any time. Chasity knew that Tommy came to put in work, so she prepared her mind for the task of getting fucked hard. He took his clothes off and put his stiff penis in her mouth and shoved it down her throat. She moaned in protest, but she didn't stop him from manhandling her. There was something about his roughness that Chasity enjoyed. He didn't treat her like the doll she appeared to be. Tommy treated her like the thot he knew she was. And Chasity loved it.

For fifty-five minutes straight, Tommy pummeled her vagina before ejaculating and leaving her sore. "I'll see you next week, same time." Tommy was a man of few words. He was dressed and out the door minutes after he was done.

Chasity had twenty minutes before her next appointment, and she wasn't ready. She dragged her sore body to the bathroom and took a long, hot shower. As she rubbed her vagina, she thought about her first trick, Vinny. *I knew Vinny was a breadwinner! What if I can entice Vinny to the point where he'll just take care of me, and I don't have to be fucking like this for money? It would be nice to be taken care of for a change.* She became so engrossed in her thoughts that she lost track of time.

There was a knock on the door. Her next trap was on time.

"Hold on, I'm coming!" she shouted from the shower as she got out and dried off. *Got to get this money. It's all in a day's work.* Chasity opened the door.

"Hi Paul. Come in and make yourself comfortable."

The quick arm movement in her peripheral disrupted Chasity's recollection. Detective Colon paused the video. "So, you met Vinny on the Front Page website." A beat passed before she spoke again. "I'm going to do you a favor."

"What's that?"

"I'm not going to arrest you for prostitution. Let's just pretend like I don't know anything about that. I'll erase the whole first part when we're done, so we both won't get into hot water."

Detective Colon pushed record on the video. "Continue." *Murderous slut! You just couldn't keep your fucking cunt-hole closed!*

CHAPTER 2

No Honor Among Thots!

Construction Site

Dix Hills, Long Island

Yo, I'm telling you, man. This chick was gorgeous with a body like a goddess!" Vinny took a pill bottle containing the opiate Oxy and popped one as he spoke to his cousin, Rocco.

"You need to take it easy on the candy." Rocco was referring to the blue pill Vinny just popped.

"I need it for my back pain; this shit is killing me lately."

"I'm just saying, it's easy to get hooked on those things." Rocco shook his head as he spoke. "Anyway, you said you found her on that website."

"Yeah, Front Page. She goes by the name Cherry. Her pics do her no justice. She looked okay, but in person she was dynamite!" Vinny smiled just thinking of her. "I'm not sharing this one with you this time. She's all mine," he said in a serious tone. In the past they shared prostitutes.

"Well, let me know if she has a friend or something. I'll fuck around a little. By the way, how's Jenny and the kids?" Rocco asked.

"She's okay. The kids are driving me nuts with their bullshit. I bust my ass so that they'll have everything, and they still get into trouble. I'm going to court right now because Anthony stole clothes from the mall. Funny thing was, he had a pocket full of money when they caught him." Vinny shook his head just thinking about his troubles at home.

"We did worse when we were his age. Sounds like he needs attention or something."

"Then you wonder why I need Cherry's services. In fact, I'm going to see her when this job is done."

"You've been seeing her every day. She must have some good pussy. You can't get enough."

"I just met her last week . . . I can't explain how she makes me feel. It's like she's dedicated to pleasing me to the utmost, Rocco. I could marry this broad, I'm telling you. 'Ho or no 'ho, I love this chick."

Rocco frowned and shook his head. "Now you're talking crazy, Vinny!"

"It's my life, and I can do what I want," Vinny spoke calmly

"You have a wife and kids. You can't throw that away for some two-bit slut you met online at some prostitution website!" Rocco fumed.

"If you have a problem with it, you don't have to fuck with me!" He got in Rocco's face.

"Oh yeah! So you're going to choose some cunt over your own flesh and blood?" Rocco pushed Vinny in his chest with both hands. Vinny stumbled two steps back.

"If that's how you want to put it!" Vinny replied, catching his balance.

"Fuck you, Vinny! One day you're going to eat those words!" Rocco stormed off and hopped into his Ram truck and sped off from the construction site, leaving a small dust storm in his wake.

"Fuck me! No, fuck you!" Vinny took out his phone and dialed Cherry.

****

"Suck that dick! Oooo! That shit feels sooo good!" Sincere said while Chasity gave him fellatio.

As she was performing, her cell phone went off. She saw that it was Vinny. Without taking her mouth off Sincere's penis, Chasity answered the phone with one hand while holding his dick with the other.

"Hello, Cherry?" Vinny said like an excited teen.

She removed Sincere's penis from her mouth. "Hey, baby," she said those two words, then put his dick back where it had been.

"I need to see you."

"Mm-kay."

"Can I come by like right now?" Vinny asked in a desperate tone.

"Sure . . ." She quietly slurped Sincere's pole in between words. ". . . I'm here, baby." She continued sucking.

Sincere had to muster the strength not to make a noise because he wanted to moan in ecstasy. He knew he had to keep his composure, so he closed his eyes and covered his mouth with one hand.

"I'll be there in twenty minutes."

"Okay, baby . . ." She sucked it one hard time before speaking again. "I'm going to get freshened up for you." She hung up.

"Yeah! I like that freaky shit! Talking on the phone while sucking on that cock! Ooo, you so nasty!" Sincere was close to ejaculating.

"We have to cut this shit short today, Sincere."

"What you mean? I gave you a whole ounce of loud for my usual hour. If you cutting my time in half, I'm giving you half an ounce!"

"Shut up and nut in my mouth!" She took him to the back of her throat, nearly swallowing him. "There it goes!"

Sincere filled Chasity's mouth up with warm cream. "Ooo! And you swallow! You so nasty!"

"Now get your ass out of my room!" she demanded.

"I was just playing. You can keep the whole ounce. You always take care of the god. For real!" Sincere pulled up his pants and then buckled his belt. "I'll see you next week, and we can square off with that extra half an hour," he said as he stood outside the door.

"Whatever, Sincere!" She slammed the door in his face.

Chasity rolled up a gigantic blunt of Sincere's top shelf marijuana and lit it up. She grabbed the bottle of Henny lying on the dresser and guzzled it. It took three more pulls of the blunt, then another swig before the room started spinning. Satisfied with the desired effect, she smiled and grabbed her laptop.

"Damn, a bitch got four new traps! This shit don't stop! My shit stay lit!" She turned on the radio and Bobby Shmurda's "Hot Nigga" played on the airwaves. Chasity turned the volume up to maximum capacity.

"Hey! Hey!" she shouted, doing the signature '*shmoney dance*' that went with the song. "I send a little thot/to get the drop on 'em!" She sang along with Bobby to her favorite part of the song.

A few minutes later, she put the blunt out and quickly took a shower before Vinny got there. Like clockwork, Vinny was at the door knocking with flowers in his hand. Chasity opened the door wearing nothing but a lace bra and panties.

"Hey baby!" Chasity paused. "You brought me flowers! You're so sweet, Vinny."

Vinny handed her a dozen long-stemmed red roses while blushing. "It's the least I can do for the most beautiful girl in the world."

"You're going to make me cry." Chasity was fronting. She really wanted to laugh. *This nigga is a sucker with a capital S!*

"I was thinking, instead of us having sex, I'd like to take you to a fancy Italian restaurant for dinner," Vinny said nervously. He wasn't sure how she'd respond.

"I am kind of hungry. Sure, let's go to dinner."

"Great!" Vinny's eyes lit up and he smiled. "I'll wait for you in the car."

While Vinny was in the car he popped a pill. Whenever he was nervous he'd use the powerful drug to calm his nerves.

Chasity got dressed and waltzed out to Vinny's car. "Nice car, Vin!" Vinny opened the passenger door for Chasity, and she eased onto the leather seat.

"You like it?" he asked once he returned to the driver's seat.

"I love it! This is the new BMW 650i convertible. Who wouldn't love it?"

"It's yours." Vinny looked at her with a serious expression.

"You're joking, right?" Chasity didn't find it funny.

"I'm as serious as cancer. I have six cars. It's nothing for me to give you this one if it makes you happy."

Chasity hugged him tight. "Oh, Vinny! I can't believe it!"

"Believe it, doll face! If it makes you happy, then it's yours."

"I don't know what to say." Chasity was at a loss for words.

"You can start with 'Thank you, Vinny.'" Vinny smiled, then started the car and began driving toward their destination.

When they arrived at Mama Leona's, Chasity was smiling from ear to ear. She looked at her new BMW once she made her exit. Slowly, she walked around it, examining every curve. She still couldn't believe Vinny just gave her a BMW. *I'm going to stunt hard in this fucking car! Haters beware!*

Vinny watched her admiring the vehicle. "Anything to make you happy, doll face."

They strolled into Mama Leona's like they owned the place. It was a traditional Italian restaurant with portraits of Italy on the walls and dim lights. They were seated in a cozy booth. The waitress came and they placed their orders. Of course, Chasity had to have alcoholic drinks with her meal. Vinny didn't mind, he was in heaven just being in Chasity's presence.

The food arrived and Chasity dug in like an inmate just set free. "You really were hungry," Vinny said, noticing her eating frenzy.

"No, it's not that. I was smoking some good weed right before you came, so I'm hungry because of that."

"I was thinking, maybe you should move into one of my condos. It's a gated community, so no one gets in without your permission. You'll be safer that way. I worry about you staying in those cheap hotels every night."

"Aww, you're the best, Vin!" She grabbed his hand and squeezed it. "No man has ever cared about me this much." Fake tears slid down her cheeks.

"Don't cry, baby." Vinny was sincerely touched. He took a napkin and gently wiped her cheeks. "It's the least I can do for the woman that makes me feel like a million bucks every day."

"I really don't know what to say."

"Say you'll move your stuff in tomorrow."

"Okay, I'll move my stuff in tomorrow." She smiled and that sealed the deal.

An hour and a half later, the two finished eating. On the way to the car, Vinny passed her the keys to the BMW. "You drive."

Chasity jumped in the driver's seat and started up the expensive vehicle. The engine growled when she pressed the gas pedal. She got moist just feeling the car's power.

"Where do you want me to go?" she asked.

"You can take me home, and I'll see you tomorrow." Vinny gazed at her with infatuation in his eyes.

Chasity adjusted the seats to accommodate her long legs. "You're dead serious about giving me this car, aren't you?"

"I surely am."

"What do you want in return for the car?" Chasity knew the car came with a price.

"I just want you to be mine when you're with me. I know what you do and I respect it. All I ask is when you're with me to treat me like the only man in the world, and I'll be cool with that."

"So let me get this straight. As long as I treat you like my man, you're okay with what I do for a living?" She was confused because no man would wife a thot.

"Exactly!" Vinny said with enthusiasm.

"Okay, you got a deal." Chasity hugged him and kissed him passionately on his lips.

The kiss shocked him. "Wow! That was a great kiss. May I have another?"

"You sure can." This time she stuck her tongue all around his mouth.

"I can get used to this." Vinny was as jovial as a kid in a candy shop.

Vinny showed her where to drop him off, and she drove back to her room. When she pulled up, Kat was standing in the doorway to her room watching Chasity get out of the BMW.

"Whose car is that?" Kat asked as Chasity approached her.

"It's mine." Chasity tilted her head smugly. "Just got it from Vinny."

"Are you serious!"

"He just gave it to me after he took me to dinner at Mama Leona's."

"I love Mama Leona's! I'm hatin' right now!"

"Bitch! Don't hate, congratulate!" Chasity ran her hands through her hair and turned her head from side to side. "I got some bomb ass loud from Sincere today. You want to smoke?"

"Hell yeah! I didn't smoke nothing all day."

They walked in the room and started smoking and drinking the rest of the Henny.

"Guess what?" Chasity asked.

"Let me see . . . homeboy is buying you a house?" Kat rolled her eyes.

"Close. He's moving me into a condo tomorrow."

"Damn! This guy is serious. See if he has a friend or something. I'm trying to come up too," Kat said.

"I most definitely will ask him if he has a guy friend for you."

"Let me know."

They smoked and drank until they both passed out on Chasity's bed. When Chasity was completely out, Kat got up and looked at her phone. She saw Vinny's number and she memorized it and put it into her phone. *You're not the only one that can throw it down on a trap,* Kat thought as she went to her room. She thought about calling Vinny, but decided against it. *I'll just call him tomorrow after Chasity leaves.*

She almost felt guilty about snaking Chasity, but that feeling passed quickly. *Just like there's no honor among thieves, there's no honor among thots either.*

CHAPTER 3

Promoted!

Fairfield Condos

To put it bluntly, Chasity had just got promoted in life. After two short months of knowing Chasity, Vinny kept his promise and moved Chasity into his condo. She came with nothing but a suitcase full of clothes. The whole condo was already beautifully furnished with an eggshell white leather couch in the living room and glass end tables. A 70-inch flat screen TV hung from the wall. The bedroom was even more captivating. The balcony overlooked a manmade lake nestled in the middle of the complex.

"This is beautiful, Vinny!" She hugged him tight. "How could I ever repay you?"

"Well, you can start by giving me a blowjob."

"I thought you'd never ask." Chasity did what she does best. When she was done, Vinny went to sleep, leaving her to think about her new condo. Never in her life had she dwelled in anything this lavish before. Chasity came from a poor family with no father. She had two sisters she didn't get along with because Chasity fucked both of their men, which led to her being excommunicated from the family.

Her mother, Catherine, was an alcoholic and didn't care about her daughters. They were left to fend for themselves. That's how Chasity ended up in the streets selling her body. She was introduced to prostitution at the early age of sixteen by an older girl named Nancy. Nancy taught Chasity everything she knew about the sex trade. When Nancy got arrested for boosting, Chasity stepped her game up and became the thot that she was.

As Chasity reflected on her past, shivers shot up her spine. One incident always haunted her. When Chasity was nine years old, her uncle Tony molested her. This went on for three years, until Tony was locked up for attempted murder. If he hadn't gotten arrested, he would still be sexually abusing young Chasity.

During that time, Chasity tried to tell her mother about her Uncle Tony, but she dismissed her daughter as a liar. "Stop lying on my brother! You know damn well he didn't do anything to your little nasty ass!" her mother stated.

"I'm not lying! Every night he sneaks into my room and he rapes me! And you don't believe me! Why would I make that up?" Chasity would plead with her mother to stop Tony, to no avail.

Right now, Chasity needed a drink just thinking about her uncle Tony. Her body shook as if she were about to have a stroke.

Detective Colon stopped the recorder. "Are you all right?" she asked. "I'm sorry to hear that happened to you."

"It's okay. I needed to get it out. I've only told two people, that's my mother and now you." Chasity stared directly into Detective Colon's brown eyes.

"So, can you skip to the part where you met Torian? How did you meet Torian Berk?" Detective Colon pressed the record button again, certain her lie would come within the next three minutes.

****

There was no alcohol in the condo, so Chasity took a ride to the liquor store to get her favorite, Hennessy. She decided to go to the liquor store in the hood to stunt in her new BMW.

When she pulled up, eight black men were standing in front of the store selling drugs. Everyone in her neighborhood knew her, so heads turned when she pulled up in the new whip.

Her weed supplier, Sincere, was one of the eight men standing in front of the store. He was the first to approach her.

"What's up, Cherry? Whose BMW?" Sincere asked.

"Mine," she responded.

"Yeah right, and I'm President Obama."

"Whatever, Sincere. You know I don't be frontin'. You better act like you know!" Chasity was feeling herself.

"Okay, you moving up in the world!"

"Something like that."

She exited the car and entered the liquor store, grabbing the biggest bottle of Henny they had. Once she made her purchase, she walked out to her car. A gentleman pulled up next to her in a BMW just like hers, but it was white with 22-inch rims. She studied the car with admiration. Then she glanced at the driver and was immediately attracted to him and vice versa. *This nigga is fly as hell.*

"Nice car," he said.

"Yours is better. I like your rims," she responded.

"I can get chrome rims for the low at my boy's shop."

"How much?" she asked.

"About $2,600 for something like these."

"Okay, that's a good price."

"Take my number. My name is Torian. Lock me in." He winked.

"I most definitely will. I'm calling you now. My name is Cherry."

"Okay, Cherry. I look forward to hearing from you."

"No doubt, Torian. You will hear from me this week."

Chasity watched Torian walk into the bodega. Torian was one of the most handsome guys she'd seen in a while. She didn't get open that easily, but she was a sucker for a pretty face. And Torian had that and a muscular body to match. *I wonder what he does for a living. Whatever it is, he's getting money!*

Her ringing cell phone brought her out of her thoughts.

"Hello!" she said in an annoying tone.

"It's me. Vinny. Where are you?"

"I went to the liquor store."

"I almost panicked when I woke up and you weren't there."

Sounds like a stalker now, Chasity thought. "No need to panic. I'm not going nowhere." She pictured Torian in her head. "I'm on my way back to the condo now."

"Okay, see you in a minute."

She hung up. One thing Cherry hated was to feel smothered by a man. She would deal with it because of the car and the condo, but she had to lay down some rules and boundaries. She knew how to play him. *He's like silly putty in my hand.*

What was most on her mind was Torian. She already liked him, and all they had was a brief conversation. Torian was the type of man she could see herself in a committed relationship with, if not for her present occupation. Her one and only serious relationship had been with a man named Benji, who'd broken her heart by messing with her best friend. Ever since then, Chasity vowed to never fall in love again. With Torian, falling in love wasn't a real concern for her. Although she was highly physically attracted to him, she was nobody's fool. But then again, that's how it all starts, with the physical. Next thing you know you're in love.

When she got back to the condo, Vinny was lying on the bed watching the TV show *Cops*.

"I hate that show," she said, entering the bedroom.

"I can change it. I watch it 'cause my—" Vinny stopped mid-sentence and changed the subject. "I missed you."

"What were you about to say?" she asked, noticing the quick change of topic.

"Nothing. My brother is a cop, that's why I watch this show."

"Your brother is a pig?"

"Yes, he's a pig."

Chasity went to the bathroom as nature called. Vinny opened the door while she was sitting on the toilet to tell her something and she lost it.

"Damn! Can I go to the bathroom in peace?" she yelled.

"I'm sorry, babe." He quickly shut the door.

She finished using the bathroom and stormed out, putting one hand on her hip before addressing him.

"Listen, I'm going to have to lay down some ground rules. First of all, I don't like *no* man that needs to know where I am at all times, like I'm on parole or something. Second, when I go to the bathroom, that's the only place in this condo that I want to go alone. That's one of my biggest pet peeves."

"Okay, I'm sorry, babe. I'll never do it again. And I'll try to not treat you like you're on parole. You're funny."

Same thing that can make you laugh can make you cry. For some reason just then, Vinny repulsed her. Chasity looked at his short, fat appearance and frowned. His dress code wasn't what she liked. He wore black slacks and a white button up that was too tight. She failed abundantly at even trying to hide her expression.

"Babe, are you all right?" Vinny asked, noticing her countenance.

Chasity shook her head no. "I'm just not feeling good right now. I think I'm getting my period," she lied, needing an excuse for the moment.

"I'm going to give you a little space for a couple of days. Is that okay?"

"That's fine, baby." She kissed him on his forehead. "I'm sorry if I made you feel unwanted. It's not that. I just gotta have my personal time, that's all."

"It's okay. I understand." Vinny moped his way toward the door. "I'll see you in a couple of days." He turned back with his mouth downturned and eyes full of sadness. "See you later." Getting no response, Vinny walked out the door, hoping he hadn't pushed her too far away.

Chasity wanted to laugh. *Pitiful*. She felt no sympathy for Vinny. Nothing made her happier than not having to see him for two days. As soon as Vinny was gone, she called Torian.

"Hello?" he answered on the first ring.

"Hey, Torian."

"What's up, Cherry?"

"I was wondering if you wanted to hang out with me tonight."

"Of course. Where you want to meet?"

A cop opened the interrogation room door, interrupting Chasity's recorded interview. "Detective Colon, Lieutenant Hank wants to see you in his office for a minute."

"Excuse me, I'll be right back." Detective Colon got up and left the room. *Sonofabitch!*

****

Furious about the interruption, Detective Colon stormed into Lieutenant Hank's office and slammed the door. "What the hell was that, Lieutenant? She was almost about to tell me what I needed to know!" Detective Colon was fuming as she spoke.

"Who the *hell* do you think you're talking to, Detective!" he fired back with venom in his tone, which caused Detective Colon to calm down. "Listen, I can't have you doing this. It's against the department's policy," Lieutenant Hanks said sternly.

"I know . . . I just need to know. Aren't I entitled to know, considering the circumstances?"

"I'll give you thirty more minutes and that's it! Now go and make the most of it."

Detective Colon walked back to the interrogation room, closed her eyes, and sighed before entering. "Where were we?"

She pressed record, ready to steal more testimony from Chasity "Cherry" Tommyson. Detective Colon wasn't sure what she'd do with the information once they got down to the specifics.

Little did Chasity know, whatever she revealed from this point on could end her life, or save it. Detective Colon needed enough evidence to pin any charge on Chasity for her involvement in this double homicide.

CHAPTER 4

Here We Go!

Earth to Chasity!" Chasity jumped to attention as Detective Colon rudely interrupted her daydream, which was more like a nightmare.

"Damn! You'd think that you would have a little more consideration for me. I just saw two men that I cared for kill each other." Chasity's eyes welled up with tears. "So yeah, I'm not all here right now." The tears rolled down her cheek, and she rubbed them off with the back of her hand.

"I didn't mean to seem insensitive." *You have to fake it. Come on, Jennifer!* Detective Colon thought. "I know you've had a rough time." She grabbed her hand and held it. "If you want to stop, it's okay."

Chasity took a deep breath. "I need to get this off my chest anyway."

Detective Colon pressed record. "Whenever you're ready."

******

"Hello, Torian?" Chasity asked. "I can't see your name because I cracked the screen on my iPhone."

"Yeah, it's me, baby." The sound of Torian's voice made her moist. "I was thinking about taking you to Atlantic City for the weekend."

"Damn, aren't you speedy?" She actually liked the idea. "What's going on there besides gambling and partying?"

"Well, it actually happens to be my birthday weekend, the weekend of July 4th. My homie and his girl wanted to take me out there as a gift. I didn't want to be the third wheel, so I thought maybe I'd ask you."

Chasity was flattered. "Aww, that's sweet, Torian! What time you picking me up?"

"We leaving tomorrow at six p.m. sharp. I'll pick you up from wherever you want me to."

Chasity thought fast. She knew Vinny would get suspicious immediately.

"I got a better idea. Since it's your birthday, why don't you let me chauffeur you in my car?"

"Are you sure?"

"Positive. Besides, I never drove to Atlantic City before." She was telling the truth.

"Okay. Bet! I hope you're not one of those crazy female drivers," Torian said, hesitant about letting Chasity drive him all the way to Atlantic City.

"Trust me, boo-boo, I got you!" Chasity said, as if it were an actual fact.

"All right. See you tomorrow. I'll text you the address to pick me up at."

"Have a nice evening, Torian. See you tomorrow." Chasity hung up.

She smiled at her reflection. "You're such a fucking *thot*!"

Chasity loved to live life fast, so this was right up her alley. She'd just met Torian a week ago. Since then, she'd only spoken with him on the phone three times. They both felt that physical attraction from the first day, and they connected mentally over the phone. Now it was time to see if they had the sexual attraction. On the latter, Chasity didn't like to waste any time. *Now the only thing I have to deal with is Vinny. I can make up a fantastic story to get away from him.*

At that moment, Vinny waltzed into the condo.

Thinking of the devil, she thought as he approached her with his arms spread for a hug followed by a kiss.

"Hi, babe. Couldn't wait to see you today."

"I was just thinking about you too, baby," she replied. *I hate that he has a key to the condo, but it is part of the agreement.* She knew Vinny had to feel as if he was in a real relationship, or this arrangement wouldn't work.

"Oh yeah, what were you thinking about me?" Vinny asked.

"I want to go out of town to see my mother. I just got a call from my sister, and my mother is in the hospital."

"Sorry to hear that, babe. What's wrong? I hope it's nothing terminal." Vinny was truly concerned.

"She had the sugar, you know diabetes. She might need surgery." Chasity had to make up something that sounded truthful.

"What type of operation is she getting?"

"She might have her leg amputated." She held her head down as if she would shed tears, but she really wanted to burst out laughing. *Keep it together, girl.*

Vinny quickly held her. "It's all right, babe. I'm here for you." He held her head against his chest. "Do you want me to come?"

"No, baby, it's okay." *That's the last thing I want.*

"You sure?"

"Yes. I need to see my family alone. It's been a while since I saw them, so I need to spend time with my sisters too. Next time I'll bring you."

"I'll hold you to it." He kissed her on the forehead. "Oh yeah! I have some great news!"

"What's that, baby?" She knew anytime Vinny had great news it involved money.

"I just put in a bid for my company to win a contract worth over $30 million." Vinny was ecstatic.

"That's awesome, baby!" Just the mention of $30 million made Chasity hug and kiss Vinny. It had the desired effect, because he started grinning from ear to ear.

"If I get this contract, you don't have to work another day in your life. I just want you to myself."

"If you want me all to yourself, it's not going to be cheap, Vinny." She kissed his lips and grabbed his manhood simultaneously.

"I didn't expect it to be, trust me." Vinny was already aroused.

"Cause you know a mouth like this is priceless." She went down on Vinny and did her routine. It never failed, Vinny ejaculated in two minutes.

"Damn! No matter how hard I try, I can't stop myself from coming when you suck it." Vinny was half embarrassed about his premature ejaculation. The other part of him blamed it on Chasity's superior skills. Which was a good thing.

"Can I have some money for my trip?" She wiped semen from her mouth as she spoke.

"Of course." Vinny pulled out a wad and peeled off thirty crisp hundred dollar bills. "Here you go, babe. That's $3,000, which should take care of everything. Buy your mom a gift and tell her it's from Vinny."

"Vinny, you're the best!" She hugged and kissed him passionately. "When I come back I'm going to put this tight, young pussy all over that dick!"

"I can't wait!"

"I'm going to get ready for my trip." She kissed him and parted ways, jumping in her BMW headed for Nordstrom's, and tomorrow, her secret rendezvous with Torian.

THOT

****

Chasity pulled up to the address Torian sent her in the text. He stood by his BMW looking at his phone. He was dressed immaculately in a Givenchy shirt and jeans with Giuseppe Zanotti sneakers. "Hey, birthday boy!" she said as she jumped out and hugged him. She handed him a package. "This is for you. Happy Birthday, Torian!"

He opened it, and when he saw the new Versace cologne he was ecstatic. "Wow! I was just looking at this in Nordstrom's. You paid a grip for this! Thank you, Cherry!"

"It's nothing." She locked eyes with him. *Damn you look good.*

"You ready to roll?" she asked, breaking the ice from the awkward moment.

"We have to wait for my boy Sincere to roll up, and then we out."

Did he just say Sincere? I hope it's not goofy ass Sincere that I get my weed from. Her hopes had failed her because sure enough, lo and behold, Sincere pulled up in his dark blue Lexus with a girl in the passenger seat.

Oh my god! Why? Why did his homie have to be nasty ass Sincere? This is going to be crazy!

Sincere noticed Chasity off the top. He almost crashed into her BMW from the reaction. *Oh shit! That's freaky ass Cherry! I know this fool ain't bringing her on this trip!*

"What's up, my G?" Torian said to Sincere as he got out the car to greet him with their signature handshake.

"You, that's what's up. Happy Birthday, Tee!" Sincere and Torian were childhood friends.

"You ready to act up? You ready to turn up, my nigga?" Torian was already amped, and the party hadn't even begun.

"I'm ready!"

"Hi, Sincere." Chasity decided to break the ice and greet him first.

"I thought that was you! Hey, Cherry. How you been?" They both pretended like their encounters weren't debaucheries.

"Still promoting parties." She winked.

"Oh yeah? That's what's up." Sincere caught on quickly. *This bitch be promoting all right, but it don't be no fucking parties.*

Torian was oblivious to the truth and actually happy that his best friend knew a girl that he was considering taking serious. Torian was really feeling Chasity. When he thought about her, he could see himself with her in a serious relationship. First, he had to get the low down from his best friend. He knew he could count on Sincere for sound advice. Or at least he thought so. Torian could trust Sincere with anything, but when it came to women Sincere was a snake. Torian's charm with the ladies was the one thing Sincere envied about him.

"Let's get this show on the road," Sincere announced.

Torian hopped in the BMW with Chasity, and they were off to Atlantic City for a weekend of fun.

Chasity had a heavy foot, so she mashed the pedal right after she crossed the Verrazano Bridge.

"Damn, girl! Slow down!" Torian protested. "I'm not trying to be in ICU on my birthday!"

"Relax, boo-boo! I got you!" She turned up the radio. "This my song! These 'hos ain't loyal!" She rocked back and forth to Chris Brown singing his ode to unfaithful females.

Torian reclined his seat back and got comfortable. "Fuck it! If tonight's my night to die, so be it."

Chasity opened the middle console and pulled out a freshly rolled blunt of kush mixed with sour. "Spark that up, shorty!" she yelled over the music.

Torian lit the blunt and inhaled a healthy pull. He coughed as he exhaled. "You my type of bitch, Cherry!" He took two more pulls and passed the blunt to her.

She held on to the steering wheel with one hand and grabbed the blunt with the other one and inhaled almost an equal amount as Torian. Then she passed it back.

"You my type of nigga." She winked and licked her lips.

The gesture made Torian's nature rise. He studied Chasity as she smoked and drove at the same time. It was something about her independent prowess that drove him wild. The way she took control of the situation put him at ease. Although it was contrary to the fact that he was always in control. Still, he found their encounter intriguing. *I need a bitch like Cherry in my life.*

Having Chasity in his life wasn't a problem, if not for his wife and two kids, who lived in their three-bedroom high ranch in Brentwood. Torian liked to have his cake and eat it too. No matter the cost. He knew Tondra would flip out if she knew he was taking another woman to Atlantic City for his birthday. Just like a true gambler, Torian rolled the dice.

"So tell me about yourself?" Torian asked. "I mean like, how old are you? What's your mama's name? How many brothers and sisters do you have? That kind of stuff."

"Damn! What's this, Twenty Questions or something?" She rolled her neck. "I'm just playing with you."

"I was about to say, 'shorty is anti-social or something,'" Torian replied.

"I have two sisters. I've never met my father, and I'm twenty-three years young. With no kids and no responsibilities, other than looking fly and getting this money!" Chasity liked to keep it simple.

"Okay, I feel you." The more they conversed, the more attracted Torian became.

"What about you? Do you have any kids? What do you do for a living? If you don't mind me asking." Chasity knew that guys didn't like to divulge their business if it was illegal.

"I have two boys. Jamony is five, and Torian Jr. is seven."

"Are you with the mother of your children?" Chasity asked, hoping the answer was no. The hesitation told her the answer was yes.

"No! As my man Fab put it, 'I'm as single as a dollar bill.'" Torian was lying through his teeth. "Other than that, I'm a Young Boss Player. All I do is get fast money and live fast!" Torian made money hustling everything, from narcotics to insurance scams. You name it, he hustled it.

"Okay, I guess that sums it up. You're a drug dealer, slash hustler, slash pimp. You do it all!" She was being sarcastic.

"I'm just a Young Boss Player. That's it."

"I heard that before, Young Boss Player. Is that a set of a gang or something?" she asked curiously.

"It's not a set of a gang. It's just an organization or a brotherhood, so to speak. It's just basically a group of young black entrepreneurs that hold each other down and come together for one common cause."

"And what's that?"

"To get money!"

They made small talk all the way there, so they arrived at Atlantic City in no time. They checked into their rooms and hit the casino. Torian was a gambler, and he played all the games from poker to roulette. Sincere was more of the blackjack guy, spending all of his time playing at his slow pace. While the guys gambled, Chasity got to know Sincere's companion, Mocha.

"How long you been with Torian?" Mocha asked.

"I'm not with him at all. I've known him all of one week. But I do like his swag, and he is real cute and everything, so you know . . ." Chasity couldn't help but blush when talking about Torian.

"I've been on and off with this fool Sincere for about ten years now. No commitments! I like it better that way. We both know where we stand."

"I know that's right." Chasity slapped her five.

Mocha was an older woman who just got better with time. You couldn't really tell her age, you just knew from her child bearing hips that she'd been around. Thick in all the right places, including ass and tits, even her lips were thick, which made her look sexual at all times. Her skin was the color of her name, a creamy mocha spread evenly.

"Let me tell you something." Mocha stared Chasity in her eyes. "Get what you can get out of these niggas. 'Cause all they want to do is jump up and down in your guts with their dicks. If you're going to have a sore pussy, at least get something out of it."

"My sentiments exactly!" Chasity replied.

"So listen, me and you are going to play the game together. Let's show these boys a real good time tonight."

Mocha wasn't quite sure if Chasity got the meaning, but she would later on.

When the guys were finished gambling, it was time to retire.

"How'd you do on the blackjack table?" Torian asked Sincere.

"Not so good. I lost about a stack," Sincere replied.

"I'm up a stack."

"Better you than me. After all, it is your birthday."

"Let's smoke and drink in my room," Torian offered.

"Cool! We'll meet you in your room."

The guys parted ways and went looking for their dates, ready to see what else the night had awaiting them.

****

Torian and Chasity sat on the bed. Chasity rolled up a blunt, while Torian took out some crystal looking substance.

"What's that?" Chasity asked.

"This is molly. The good stuff—not that garbage." As he was crushing it up, Sincere knocked on the door. "Come in, my G!"

Sincere opened the door and saw Torian crushing up the molly. "That's what I'm talking about, my G! Let's get it rollin' in this bitch!"

"Word! I been waiting to get my roll on all night!" Mocha said with excitement.

That's what she was talking about when she said we going to show these boys a good time tonight. They're all on molly, Chasity thought. *I've never done that shit before in my life.*

They all took the molly and put it into their own water bottles. Torian made a bottle for Chasity. She looked at the bottle, then at Torian.

"I don't know about this. I've never done molly before," Chasity stated.

"It's just like smoking weed. It makes you feel good," Torian explained.

"It's like smoking ten blunts!" Mocha chimed in.

"Word! And you know I smoke mad trees!" Sincere reassured.

"Okay. Fuck it! I'm in!" Chasity took the bottle and gulped down half of it.

"Slow down, champ!" Torian said with concern. "You just started, take it easy."

"You right."

It was too late. The effects of the pure molly had already started making its way into her blood stream. Her senses began to tingle. Suddenly, she became extremely horny and gazed at Mocha with pure lust. So she grabbed her ass and then her tits. Mocha responded by kissing

Chasity on her lips, then sticking her tongue into her mouth.

The guys noticed the girls playing with each other, so they joined in. Torian began fondling Chasity's breasts and ass while Sincere did the same to Mocha. Torian ripped Chasity's clothes off and stared at her body with lust.

"That's what I'm talking about!" Sincere said, ripping Mocha's clothes off. Mocha had so many stretch marks on her stomach it looked like a Bengal tiger. Nevertheless, she was still sexy.

Chasity's body was perfect. No stretch marks, just even-toned, yellow skin. She almost glowed. Both men were in awe of her body; even Mocha was caught in a trance. They all rubbed and touched Chasity as if she were a marvel to the world. The glitter lotion she used added to the allure they were experiencing from the powerful narcotic.

"Wow! Look at her body!" Mocha said.

"I know. I never seen nothing like it before in my life," Sincere stated.

"Me either. She looks like an angel!" Torian added.

They all began caressing and kissing her. She was creaming all over herself with each touch. She wanted to be penetrated. She couldn't take it anymore. "Fuck me! Please somebody fuck me!" Chasity couldn't contain herself. She tried to grab Torian's dick through his zipper, but it was too big. "Damn! This is the biggest dick I ever saw in my life!" She wasn't lying about that either. Torian was well endowed.

She pulled his pants down, pulled out his penis, and sucked it so hard he yelped, "Aww! Easy!"

Sincere and Mocha were watching until Sincere went behind Chasity and pushed his dick in her vagina while she sucked Torian's dick. This left Mocha alone; both men were lured into Chasity's playhouse.

She felt Sincere entering her from behind. This turned her on past the point of no return. She moaned as she continued to give Torian fellatio. The moaning created a vibration on the head of his penis that sent him into overdrive.

"Damn, Cherry!" Torian yelled. "That shit feel good as hell!"

Sincere was enjoying her vagina. "Let me get some." Sincere spun her so he could stick his dick in her mouth, and Torian could get the wet vagina Sincere just exited.

Torian had to take his time inserting his log into her opening. "Damn, this shit is tight!"

"Aww!" Chasity moaned. "Your dick is so big!"

"You was right! Her mouth is incredible!" Sincere pretended this was his first time.

All the while Mocha just watched. "Umm, excuse me! I'm sitting here with a wet pussy and good head as well." No one responded. The guys were enamored by Chasity's sexual skills. To the point they forgot Mocha was even there.

Sincere was the first to ejaculate. "Ahh, I'm coming!" He unloaded his sperm into her mouth. Chasity swallowed every drop.

That sent Torian into warp drive. He began pounding her vagina with the strength of ten men. Losing all sense of reality, he was ensnared in a trance. He beat the brakes off her pussy.

"Stop! You're hurting me! Please!" she begged to no avail.

"Shut up!" Torian slapped her hard on her ass. "Take all this dick!" He thrust harder with each word he uttered. "I'm going to give you all this cum! You ready!"

Realizing that Torian wasn't going to stop, she just relaxed and let him beat it up. "Yes! Cum in my pussy!"

"Uhh! I'm coming!" Torian squeezed all of his juices into her vagina. When he was done he fell on the bed and closed his eyes. "Damn that was fucking good!"

Chasity closed her eyes, moaned, and took a deep breath- all in one motion. The memory of that night caused a sexual rush to her libido. She paused to regain her composure.

Detective Colon felt mixed emotions. She was turned on, and at the same time she was furious. She turned off the camera.

"You'll have to excuse me. I have to use the ladies room." She dashed to the bathroom and shut the door behind her.

"I don't know how much longer I can keep this up." She trembled as she looked at her reflection in the mirror. Bags had settled under her eyes from being up for almost twenty-four hours straight. Fatigue was starting to set in. She needed some rest. But she couldn't, not with what was going on.

"I just need to get to the bottom of this shit once and for all." She splashed cold water on her face. It gave her a jolt of awareness.

Detective Colon looked at her wristwatch, knowing she was still on the clock. "This is it. Here we go." She took a deep breath and exited the bathroom.

She entered the room then pressed record.

Chasity eased back against the chair, becoming more relaxed. So she was ready to open up.

"I'm starting to like this interrogation." Chasity smiled and nodded.

"Why would you say that?" Detective Colon asked curiously.

"This shit is very therapeutic! My home girl Kat always told me I needed to see a psych. I guess this is the next best thing." She felt a pressure release from her mind as she spoke her truth.

"If you say so," Detective Colon said while simultaneously thinking, *The only difference is that I'm not here to help you. I'm here to bury you, bitch!*

"Are you ready to continue?" Detective Colon asked with a deceptive smile.

CHAPTER 5

All the Way to the Bank!

After the expedition to Atlantic City, Torian and Chasity were like two birds of a feather. They couldn't get enough of one another. They were drawn by all the similarities in their lifestyles. The youth and beauty, the fast money, the sex. All of these elements made a volatile cocktail that was bound to explode.

Chasity had to see Torian every day, like a junky that needs a fix. She took advantage of every chance she got to get away from Vinny to spend time with Torian. She didn't care what Vinny was thinking about her many disappearing acts lately. As far as she was concerned, she had Vinny in the palm of her hand. She noticed him becoming a bit suspicious because he began to call her more often to check up on her whereabouts.

"Hello, Cherry?" Vinny thought he heard a man's voice in the background. "Who're you with?"

"What?" Chasity heard him loud and clear.

"I thought I heard somebody in the background. Like a man."

"No, silly." *Shh! S*he put her finger up to her lips for silence. Torian was rapping along with the radio. "That was just the radio. I'm in the car."

"Oh! Well, I have some good news for you! I need to see you ASAP!" Excitement filled Vinny's tone.

"Why can't you just tell me on the phone?" Chasity didn't want to leave Torian's side.

"No deal! Get your sweet ass to the condo if you want to get the gift and the news."

"Okay, I'll be there in thirty minutes." She hung up the phone.

"Sugar Daddy calls," Torian commented sarcastically.

"Shut up, big head boy!" Chasity playfully smacked the side of his head.

"Don't get mad at me because you have to go."

"Stay here. I'll be back in a few hours. I promise." She kissed him passionately on the lips. "Keep that big dick out and ready for me to suck."

"Depends on how long you take to get back." He smiled. "I might find someone else to give it to."

"Stop playing with me, Torian!" She smacked him on the side of his head again, only harder. "Don't play with me like that!" Chasity got serious.

"I was just playing, crazy ass girl!" He grabbed her up and playfully slammed her on the bed before kissing her. "Hurry up and come back."

She left the hotel suite they were in and quickly arrived at the condo. Vinny's Jaguar was in the driveway. As soon as she opened the door, there were flowers sitting on the centerpiece. There was a card placed in between the flowers that said 'read me.'

Cherry,

You've brought light into my life in such a way that I can't fathom not having you. You've made me pay attention to life itself, how beautiful it is. There's no amount of money that can compensate you for what you've done for me. This check is a start.

She looked around for the check, but there was none there. That's when her iPhone vibrated to indicate that she had a text message from Vinny. It was a screenshot from Chase bank.

The check you deposited is cleared! Thank you for using Chase bank!

Amount Available: $350,000.00

"Oh my God!" She looked around for Vinny. "Vinny! Baby, where are you?"

"I'm right here." He came downstairs.

Chasity hugged him so hard. "Thank you, baby! I can't believe you did this for me."

"You deserve it. For all that you do for me, that's the least I can do."

"What made you do this?" Chasity was curious. "I mean, it's not everyday someone deposits $350,000 into your account."

"Remember that $30 million bid I mentioned a few weeks ago?"

"Yes, I remember you mentioning it."

"Well, we won the bid! I wanted to wait until my portion of the money was given to me and my check cleared before I told you anything."

"Wow! This is incredible!" She thought about how considerate Vinny was, and how she was really playing him. All the way to the bank—literally.

Those thoughts made her shed a few tears. Usually, Chasity was hardcore when it came to Vinny. But something about this kind act weighed on her conscience. She knew how she really felt about Vinny. She didn't love him at all, not even a little bit. Especially after all the time she was spending with Torian.

"Why are you crying?" Vinny asked.

"They're tears of happiness." *I'm ready to take this money and disappear with Torian.*

"There is one condition for the money."

I knew there was some bullshit! Chasity thought. "What's that, baby?"

"You have to stop posting your services on Front Page. And dedicate yourself to me and me only," he said, his demeanor as serious as cancer.

"I think I can do that." *As long as I can still see Torian, it doesn't matter.*

"Great! Let's celebrate!"

Vinny took her to City Island, and from there they went shopping. Chasity kept looking at things to buy for Torian.

She knew his style and taste. He liked designer items just like she did. They complemented each other.

"He's definitely a size ten and better," Chasity said to herself, while looking at the beautifully crafted Buscemi designer sneakers.

Vinny walked up behind her. "I wear a size 8 ½ by the way, in case you were wondering."

This dude is always up my ass! I can't even enjoy a moment of thought about the real man I love. Chasity made an annoying gesture with her face while shaking her head.

"I was just looking at them. Not particularly for you, they're not your style." Her tone was arrogant.

"I like these. Buscemi is an Italian name, why wouldn't I like them?" Vinny said in his defense.

"Listen to you! Okay, I'll buy you these, and I want you to wear them," she commanded.

She got a text from Torian: *How much longer U have 2 play with SD?*

Chasity: *Not much longer. He is creepy sometimes. I miss U baby.*

Torian: *I'm going 2 make a run. Meet U back here l8r 2nite.*

Chasity: *What is your foot size?*

Torian: *Size 10 in Jordans, & 11 in anything designer.*

Chasity: *OK. C U l8r.*

"Who was that, baby?" Vinny asked while trying to look at her messages.

"Damn! Yo dude! Can I have some privacy?" Chasity couldn't take it anymore when she saw Vinny deliberately trying to read her messages. "That's why I don't have a man, because of shit like that."

"Well, excuse me! I give you $350,000 and that's the thanks I get." Vinny stormed away.

When he was out of her earshot she told the salesman, "Get these in a size 8 ½ and a size 11."

CHAPTER 6

I Can't Wait to Meet this Dumb Ass Bitch!

Torian pulled up to his high ranch house in Brentwood Long Island. It was all white with black trimming. Everything about the house was plush, inside and out. It was the best well-kept house on the block. His wife Tondra was looking out of the second story window when Torian pulled up in his BMW that she helped him buy. In fact, the house and everything he owned was due to Tondra's career as a Mental Health Therapist.

When Torian first met Tondra, he was a manager at Wal-Mart. He knew she was a good girl, one he had to keep. So he asked to marry Tondra right after she graduated from Stony Brook University with her Master's Degree as a Licensed Clinical Social Worker. Shortly afterward, he got her pregnant back to back with two boys. Her salary was how they were able to get the mortgage and the car loan. Without her 850 credit score, Torian would be driving something American instead of the foreign car he currently drives. He owed it all to his wife, Tondra, but she felt like he was taking advantage.

As soon as he walked in, she gave him the business. "We need to talk." Those were Tondra's first words.

Torian flopped down on the butter soft cream leather couch. "Let's talk." His cell phone slipped out of his jacket pocket onto the couch from his jerky movement. Tondra averted her attention from it. Torian waited for her to speak.

"Ever since your birthday, you've been MIA. Are you seeing another woman?" She stared him right in his eyes. "Don't lie to me, Torian."

"No, I'm not seeing another woman. I told you I went to Atlantic City that weekend with my people. Then when I came back I had to go to Atlanta to take care of something." Torian stared right back into her eyes without blinking. He'd mastered the art of lying.

"It's just that me and the boys miss you. They ask for you every day."

Torian felt guilty about not seeing his boys. "You right. I do have to spend more time with my family." He stood up and hugged Tondra. "I miss you too, baby. I feel like it's been forever since I made love to you." Torian knew that showing her love and affection was her weak spot, something he'd been withholding as of late. Tondra was a professional working woman, but a freak nonetheless.

He pressed his penis against her vagina. "You know I can't go too long without that fucking eggplant." Tondra's nickname for Torian's penis.

"Hold that thought. Let me go use the bathroom." Torian dashed to the bathroom leaving his cell phone lying on the couch.

Tondra quickly grabbed the phone and cracked his code to unlock his phone. She had found out his code long ago—his birthday. Torian was so self-centered it wasn't hard for Tondra to figure it out. She went straight to his messages and saw recent texts from someone named Chasity. She read them all very quickly; then she memorized her number and threw his phone back on the couch where she found it. She stored Chasity's number in her phone under 'Slut.'

Torian came out of the bathroom ready to do damage. "We have to get it in before the boys get out of school." He rubbed her breast with one hand while reaching for her vagina with the other, then stroking her until moisture slicked his fingers. Torian pulled his dick out and tried to stick it in her mouth.

"Oh, damn! I forgot. I have to go down to the office." She grabbed her car keys. "I'm sorry, baby. I really have to get down to the office before they close. Can I see you later?" She kissed him on the cheek and ran out the door.

"Yeah, I guess." Torian was set on giving his wife the business.

That's strange. She would take a sick day to stay home to get this dick. Oh well.

He looked around for his phone and saw it lying on the couch. "I want to get with Cherry tonight anyway."

****

"Who is this calling me?" The number was blocked. Chasity was used to getting blocked calls because of the nature of her business, so she answered it. "Hello? Cherry speaking." That's the name Torian had her stored under.

"You don't know me, but I'm Torian's sister Tondra," the unknown female said. Torian did have a sister named Tondra. Tondra was lucky that Chasity remembered the names of his siblings from the trip.

Chasity paused, wondering about the nature of the call. "Ooookay . . ."

"How're you doing? Torian told me all about you. Well, I don't want him to know that I got your number. I took it from his phone because I was curious to talk to the woman he's dating. We're really close, and my little brother usually tells me everything. But not this time. He's been so secretive lately, and I just want to get to know the lady who's got him acting so sneaky. He must be in love, and she must be someone very, very special to him."

"Do you really think so?"

"Absolutely, girl! I'm talking 'marriage material' special. And as your future sister-in-law, I want to know everything, but it has to be on the DL. Feel me?" Tondra was a master, with a Master's.

"Oh, it's all good, girl. I won't say a word. Whatever we speak about is between me and you."

"I'm so relieved. I thought you were going to reject my friendship because of the way I'm coming at you."

"No, girl! I want to get to know his family," Chasity replied. "We have something in common."

"What's that?" *We're nothing alike, you fucking slut!* Tondra thought.

"We both love your little brother."

"Oh yeah, we both *love* Torian. Of course." Tondra paused because her thoughts were racing. "I have an idea. Why don't you come over, so we can kick it and get to know each other?"

"I'm cool with that!" Chasity grinned wide, excited. "When is a good day for you?"

"Tomorrow is good, let's say around noon. We can have lunch."

"Tomorrow it is. Just text me your address."

"Okay, see you tomorrow, Cherry." She hung up the phone.

"I can't wait to meet this dumb ass bitch!" Tondra cracked a sinister smile.

CHAPTER 7

Baby I'm Home!

Chasity couldn't wait to meet with Torian's sister, or who she thought was his sister. She got dressed to the tee, with her designer Chanel boots and hat to match. It was spring, so she wore a sweater skirt set that accented her curves. She looked stunning to say the least.

"I'm that bitch!" She stared at herself in the mirror, pleased with her reflection. She glanced at her watch. "It's almost that time, don't want to be late." Chasity put the address in her navigation, which said her destination was only fifteen minutes away. She made it there in twelve minutes due to her lead foot. She parked in the driveway and got out looking like an R&B diva.

Tondra was standing in front of the window. Chasity had butterflies.

"Can you do me a favor?" Tondra said from the perch of her windowsill, "Can you park your car in my garage?" *Damn this bitch is bad though! I can't even front*, Tondra thought with a pang of jealousy.

"Sure." Chasity got back in the car and waited for the garage door to open. She pulled in and parked, then Tondra closed it. *I'm so fucking nervous*, Chasity thought. *Pull it together.*

Tondra was there to greet her downstairs at the garage door with a hug. "You can come in through this door."

Chasity embraced her, then she followed Tondra through the door and up the stairs. "Cherry. How are you doing? It's nice to finally meet you." Tondra did her best rendition of hospitality. "Come in and make yourself comfortable."

Chasity came in and looked around, admiring the African artwork that decorated the walls. "You have a beautiful home, Tondra. I love the African paintings."

"Thank you, Cherry. I try to keep it up."

"You're doing a good job," Chasity replied.

"Would you like a drink? Some lemonade or something stronger, like Henny?"

"Sure, I'll take a double shot of Henny."

Tondra poured her the powerful alcoholic beverage and sat down next to her. "So, how long have you and Torian been together?" Tondra asked coyly.

"Only a month, but it feels like a lifetime." Chasity's face became flush as she closed her eyes in bliss.

"Really?" Tondra frowned. "How so?"

"Well, we have so much in common that it just feels like I've known him for a long time."

"Where did you guys meet?"

"We met at the liquor store on Lowell Avenue. We have the same BMW, except his is white, of course. That was the initial conversation, and the rest is history." Chasity beamed.

Tondra's stomach roiled then sank. "Really? Wow! So umm . . . what did you guys do for his birthday that just passed?" she asked, knowing that any answer would hurt her deep.

"He took me to Atlantic City. We had a ball! That's when we became closer because we had time to bond."

"I see." *Keep it together, Tondra.* She took a deep breath.

Tondra looked at her watch. *The boys should be coming home from school any minute now.*

Just like clockwork, the door swung open and the sounds of four feet stomping up the steps followed. They ran straight to their rooms, quickly changed their clothes, and were on their way out the door, the older boy with a football in hand.

"That's my boys. They're so into football they couldn't wait to come in and change into their play clothes."

The interruption from the boys almost took Tondra's mind off what Chasity just said. But it was all coming back to her now.

"So, you said that Torian took you to Atlantic City for his birthday?" Tondra gulped her own saliva to keep from exploding. *This lying motherfucker told me he went with his peoples!*

"Yeah, we had an amazing time!" Flashbacks of Torian and Sincere running a train on her played in Chasity's mind, and her pussy got wet.

"It must've been something because you just went off into space just talking about it." Tondra wore a tight smile.

"I'm sorry. I was just thinking about something we did." Chasity smiled slyly.

"What? Come on, Cherry. You can tell me."

"It's nothing. It was just some freaky shit your brother made me do, that's all."

Freaky shit he made you do, I can just imagine. You look like you'll do anything, Tondra thought. *I could kill this bitch! It's not her fault she's a fucking slut!*

"Are you okay, Tondra?" Chasity asked out of concern,
caught off guard because Tondra not only became quiet but wore a maniacal expression.

Tondra shook her head and shrugged to snap out of her trance. "I'm sorry. I was just in the twilight zone. Just thinking about something from my past."

"I do that all the time. My best friend Kat always tells me that I'm a nutcase because I be in my own world . . . in my head. Know what I mean?" Chasity did her best to make this visit a good experience. The last thing she wanted was to disappoint Torian's sister.

Tondra resented this move she made. She thought it was checkmate, but all it really was, was heartbreak. She thought about everything she had done for Torian. He wasn't a bum, but he wouldn't be able to ball out without her help.

"Are you sure you're okay?" Chasity asked, noticing Tondra sinking into a bad place. Her eyes were starting to water.

"Excuse me for a minute." Tondra ran to the back of her house where her room was located and shut the door. She couldn't take it, and she cried with her face in the pillow.

"How could he continue to do this to me after all I do for him?"

*****

Chasity was left alone in the living room. *Was it something I said? Maybe it was the story of me and her brother that caused her to think about a past lover or something? Yeah, that's what it is.* Chasity didn't know what to make of it.

As she sat there trying to figure out what was going on, Torian came in. "Baby, I'm home!" he said as he climbed the steps.

That sounds like Torian. Chasity stood up.

When Torian got to the top of the stairs and saw Chasity standing there, he almost lost his breath from the shock. "Cherry!"

"Hey, baby." She walked over to hug him but his arms didn't move. "Me and your sister Tondra have been getting to know each other." Although she was happy to see Torian, his demeanor was cold, emotionless.

"What are you doing here?" he asked as if she didn't just tell him.

"I told you. Tondra invited me over. Is there a problem?" Chasity stepped back with her eyebrows narrowed in confusion.

Tondra stormed from her room and stood in the hallway glaring at Torian with red eyes that were all cried out.

"How could you do this to me?" she said directly to Torian.

Chasity looked at her, so confused she didn't know if she was talking to her or Torian. Then she looked at Torian, whose head shook in disbelief.

"Wait a minute. Did I miss something?" Chasity asked.

"Yeah, you missed a whole lot," Tondra said, wiping her tears with her hands. "Torian isn't my fucking brother. He's my husband!"

"Your husband?" Chasity didn't get it. "How is Torian your fucking husband?"

"Exactly what I said. He's not my brother, he's my husband. I tricked you, so that I can catch this piece of shit red-handed once and for all!" Tondra broke down, crying uncontrollably.

"How didn't I see it?" Chasity asked out loud.

"Because you're a stupid bitch! If you had any morals about yourself, you wouldn't have opened your legs without getting to know who you were giving yourself to! You knew my husband all of a week before you went off to Atlantic City and fucked him! I hope you enjoyed it because I'm done! I don't need this. I'm too good of a woman to take this from any man! I can have any man I want." Tondra was deeply hurt.

"Let me explain." Torian made a move to console his wife.

"Yeah, let you explain," Chasity said. "You lied to me too! When I asked you if you were with your kids' mother, you told me NO!"

"All right, I lied! To both of you." Torian came clean, staring at both of them.

"You don't have to explain anything to me anymore. I don't even want to hear any more lies. Tell them to her." Tondra ran to her room and locked the door.

Torian ran after her. "Tee! Open the door!" He twisted the doorknob.

"I see what this is! Just open the garage, and I'll be out of y'all's life!" Chasity stormed down to the garage and pressed the button to open the door. She jumped in her car and sped off to her condo.

"That's it! I'm done with ever thinking about a relationship. I'm just going to keep it the way it is. Straight cash!" Tears streamed down her cheeks, smudging her professionally done make-up.

Detective Colon stopped the recorder. She wanted to laugh out loud in Chasity's face when she heard the story on how Tondra played her. *Good for your stupid ass!*

A ringing cell phone brought Chasity out of memory lane, but the pain of the day lingered.

Detective Colon received a call. "Excuse me." She took the call in the hallway.

"Are you still there with that bitch Cherry?"

"Yeah, I just got her to tell me some things, but not what I need to know," Detective Colon replied.

"Don't stop until she tells you where the money is. After that, I want that bitch killed."

"I got you. I'm on it." Detective Colon hung up. She closed her eyes, starting to see double from the effects of extreme fatigue. "I don't know how much more of this I can take before I lose it." She opened the door and took a deep breath before entering.

CHAPTER 8

My Little Soldier Boy!

Excuse me for the interruption, Miss Tommyson," Detective Colon said, staring Chasity directly in her eyes with disdain so strong you could smell it. "Let me ask you a question."

"Whatever." Chasity rolled her eyes heavenward.

"Why did you keep messing around with Torian after you found out he had a wife and two kids?"

At that moment Chasity's senses began to tingle. She felt the hatred coming from Detective Colon from the beginning, but she ignored it. With everything that happened, she wasn't on point at first. Chasity was used to receiving a certain vibe from jealous females, but this was more intense. She stared at Detective Colon with the same intensity.

"Well?" Detective Colon said in a mock tone.

"Detective, let me ask you a question this time. What do you have against me?" Chasity asked, folding her arms.

Detective Colon squinted, tilted her head, and decided to think before speaking. *Let me start. Could it be the fact that you're a slut that makes the whole female species look bad? Or maybe the fact that one of those men is—*

"It's obvious!" Chasity's impatience got the best of her as she cut off Detective Colon's thoughts with her outburst. "Since I came in here, you've been giving me this look, as if I did something personally to you."

"I don't even know you, so how could I possibly like you or dislike you?"

"Save it. You and I both know what the deal is. Matter of fact, why am I even here? I didn't kill anyone. I'm the victim."

Detective Colon laughed, lightly at first. Then she paused and said, "You're the victim!"

"Yes!"

Detective Colon laughed again. This time it was a hearty, loud laugh. It was so loud that officers passing the interrogation room could hear a faint sound of it.

"I can't help it!" She kept laughing until tears came down her face. "You have to excuse me for laughing so hard at your pathetic, self-centered view of reality."

"Excuse me, bitch!" Chasity rolled her eyes and her neck at the same time.

"What the fuck you just call me!" the detective said.

"I didn't call you anything, yet."

Detective Colon stood and rolled her sleeves up and started pulling her hair back.

"Oh, this bitch wanna fight." Chasity stood up. "I've been fighting all my life."

That's when Detective Colon jumped across the table and landed on top of Chasity. Her chunky fists pounded

Chasity in her face. "You fucking *slut*!" Detective Colon said, punching her continuously.

"Get the fuck off of me!" Chasity rolled her body, and Detective Colon rolled with her, giving Chasity a chance to get a clean shot to the left side of her temple.

They both hopped to their feet with their fists balled in front of their face like two female boxers. Male officers began to line up in front of the two-way mirror.

"They're fighting in there!" Detective Thomas said.

Protocol was to intervene when a confrontation between a suspect and an interrogator occurred. However, this skirmish was between two beautiful women. So the men hesitated.

Detective Samuels noticed his colleagues lining up at the interrogation window. *What the hell is going on*? he asked as he quickly dashed down the hall. He saw Chasity fighting with Detective Colon. *Cherry! What the fuck are you doing in here?* He made a move to stop it.

"Aww, come on, Samuels! Let the girls get their frustration off," Detective Thomas protested.

Detective Samuels pushed him aside and entered the room. Detective Thomas felt some kind of way about being shoved like that. *What the fuck is his problem?* he thought. *He acts like he knows her or something.*

He left the door open, which allowed Detective Thomas to hear what was being said.

When Detective Samuels entered, they were both holding each other in a wrestler's stand still. Chasity had grabbed and was now pulling Detective Colon's hair when she noticed Detective Samuels.

"Tommy?" Chasity said.

"Break it up!" he said and grabbed Chasity up in his arms. Detective Colon was left shaking off the effects of being punched and having her hair pulled. He whisked Chasity out of the room while whispering, "Shh!" in her ear. He took her into his office and closed the door and locked it.

*****

But Detective Thomas witnessed the whole episode unfold. He was most concerned with Detective Samuels being overly compassionate about this suspect. The way he whisked her into his office was almost as if he was rescuing someone he knew or cared about.

Tommy? His name is Winston Samuels. Detective Thomas thought about the name he heard Chasity say when Detective Samuels entered the interrogation room.

Detective Thomas strolled to Detective Samuels' office door and stood there pretending to look at a text message, but he was really eavesdropping on the conversation going on inside.

****

"Tommy, the truck driver. Tell me you're not a fucking detective!" Chasity said while shaking her head.

"I'm not a truck driver. That was just my cover. I'm a detective, a Homicide Detective. And my name isn't really Tommy, it's Winston." He knew he was putting his career on the line by revealing his identity.

"Winston! I prefer to call you Tommy," Chasity said sarcastically.

"Whatever. What I want to know is—why are you here?"

"It's a long story." Chasity opted not to go into it.

"If you want me to help you, it's in your best interest to tell me why you're here," Detective Samuels said sternly.

"I was having sex with my lover, and someone was hiding in the closet listening. It was my fake boyfriend— the one that I was leading on and playing with his head to keep getting his money. Well, he jumped out of the closet and shot my lover. In return, my lover shot him, but they both traded shots and killed each other." She paused and looked at him. "That's why I'm here."

"Okay, but why were you and Detective Colon fighting?"

"Good question. That bitch just jumped across the table and started punching me in my face."

Detective Samuels saw the bruises on the right side of her face. "And you have no idea why?"

"She was interrogating me like I was the one that murdered those two men or something. I don't know . . . the bitch just went crazy," Chasity replied adamantly.

Detective Samuels was trying to make sense out of it. "You aren't a suspect, so why was she interrogating you? Detective Colon isn't even a Homicide Detective. She works the Narcotics Division. There's definitely something fishy about that."

"Explain it to me," Chasity asked curiously.

"First of all, it's against protocol for a Narcotics Detective to interrogate a murder suspect. Second of all, if you were a murder suspect, you would've been handed over to me because I'm the head of the Homicide Division. I assign the detectives to their respective cases." He paused. "Someone allowed this, knowing that it was against policy."

"But why? Why would someone go through the trouble of fucking with me like that when I've been through enough just witnessing that bullshit!" Chasity trembled uncontrollably.

"Relax, Cherry. You're safe now." Detective Samuels stood and held her in his arms. He closed his eyes and reminisced on all the times he had Chasity—the many positions and the ferocity with which she sucked and fucked. As he held her, his manhood began to rise.

Chasity felt his penis rubbing against her vagina. "Not now. I'm not in the mood."

"Please? For old times' sake."

Chasity grabbed his penis through his slacks and massaged it. "You did come to my rescue in there. And I could use your help to find out why they're targeting me." She unzipped his slacks and pulled his penis through the slot and dropped to her knees.

"Oh my god! I miss it so fucking much!" Detective Samuels couldn't contain himself. He forgot where he was for a moment.

"Oh yeah, you miss it. Well, come back home to mama." *Just like clay in my hand to shape and mold into my little soldier boy,* Chasity thought as she seduced Detective Samuels to the extreme.

****

Detective Thomas listened intently. Some of the words were inaudible, but the last thing he heard was loud and clear: *"Oh my god! I miss it so fucking much!"*

I wonder what the chief is missing. It sounds like he has a side chick he likes to play with. I wonder what I can do with this little tidbit of information. Let's see, I can extort him. I do want a piece of that firm, young ass I saw. Hell, why should he be the only one enjoying it? He averted his attention back to the door. This time he put his ear on the door because it was too quiet.

"Hey, Thomas! I—" Detective Colon stopped mid-sentence, seeing Detective Thomas eavesdropping on Detective Samuels. She pretended to get water at the water cooler. She knew Detective Samuels had broken up the fight. But she didn't know where he'd taken Chasity, because she was too shaken up from the fight.

Detective Thomas swiftly dashed away from the door, and Detective Samuels exited with Chasity in tow. "I'm going to take Miss Tommyson home. She's been through enough today." He escorted her to his vehicle, and they left the vicinity.

Detective Colon peeped the whole move. *Detective Thomas knows something, and I need to get it out of him.* "It's on now, slut! Oh, it's just beginning," Detective Colon said to herself.

CHAPTER 9

What Have I Become!

You can't go back to your condo because it's the scene of an ongoing investigation," Detective Samuels informed her. "You can stay at my apartment. There's nobody there but me."

"No. I prefer to go stay with my friend Kat. She's at the Bay Shore Motor Inn."

Detective Samuels headed toward the Inn. Chasity took that time to call Kat to give her a heads up.

"What's up, thot?" Chasity and Kat liked to play like that at times.

"You, thot! I heard what happened. Are you okay?" Kat asked.

"Yeah, I'm okay. I had to put the beats on this detective bitch, but other than that I'm okay."

"Where are you at?"

"Headed towards the Inn. Are you there?" Chasity asked.

"Where else would I be?"

"I'm on my way."

"See you when you get here." Kat hung up.

There was an awkward silence in the car. Samuels stole a peek at Chasity, who seemed to be in her own world.

"Are you sure you don't want to crash at my spot for a couple of days? I can take off, and we can hang out and do some fun stuff to get your mind off that horrible event." Detective Samuels was reaching by trying to get her to stay with him.

"No, not this time, baby. Maybe next time. I just want to hang with my friend tonight. You got my new number, so use it whenever you want to have a good time. Today was on me."

Detective Samuels pulled into the parking lot of the Bay Shore Inn. "I'll call you tomorrow if I find out anything."

"Thank you for everything, Tommy."

"Don't mention it."

She got out the car, and Detective Samuels watched the sway in her hips as she walked away. He drove off when she knocked on the room door. Kat answered immediately. As soon as she saw Chasity she hugged her.

"Come here, girl."

Chasity hugged her back. This was the first time she felt remorse over the loss of the two men in her life. She really loved Torian, and she saw herself trying to settle down with him one day. After a while, she even started to love Vinny. He was so good to her that it was natural that she acquired some feelings for him.

She cried as she hugged Kat. "It's going to be all right, Cherry. I know you was starting to love Torian. It's not your fault. Everything happens for a reason." Kat's words were very comforting.

"I know. It's just that I feel so terrible because I could've avoided this shit if I would've just come clean to both of them." She sat on the edge of the bed. As she spoke she sobbed.

"You know I already got the Henny and the blunt waiting on you." Kat handed her the bottle, the blunt, and a lighter. "You do the honors." Kat sat next to her on the bed.

Chasity sparked up the blunt and took a huge pull. "This is my first blunt of the day."

"Get right. You need it," Kat said.

They passed the blunt back and forth while taking large gulps of the brown water. It took every bit of an hour to finish both substances. They were both where they wanted to be—in La-La Land on cloud nine.

"I'm officially fucked up in this bitch!" Chasity said.

"Me too, my nigga."

"Let me ask you a question," Chasity said.

"Sure."

"Do you ever think about giving up this way of life and squaring up? Getting a legit job, or investing in a business?" Chasity often thought like this.

"Sometimes, but the thought of working a regular job keeps me turning tricks. I can't see working hard for eight hours and only making four to $500 a week. When I can get that in two hours. Sorry, I'll stick to what I do best," Kat said matter of factly.

"After today I had to ask myself: self, is it really all worth it? I mean, yes we make a lot of money, but it comes with a lot of bullshit too. I want to do something that I'm proud of one day, something I can tell my kids, when I have them. I don't want to live like this for the rest of my life. Eventually, we're going to get old, and no one is going to want us anymore." Chasity lay on her back staring at the ceiling.

"I'm not going to front. I never thought of it like that before. You right though. When you think about it . . ." Kat paused. "But fuck that! That just means that I have to turn up before a bitch get old. Know what I'm saying?"

"No I don't know what you're saying. Because there isn't any pension for this shit. If something happens to you, there's no worker's comp. We have nothing but the guarantee that men are going to want to fuck us now. But ten years, fifteen years from now, who knows what can happen? I'm not trying to be doing this in ten years." Chasity didn't realize how ignorant Kat really was.

Kat got a call. "Hey, baby. Of course you can come over. You know where I'm at. Just bring that big old dick to mama."

Chasity knew that was her cue to get out of the room before Kat's trap arrived. "I'm going to get a room because I can't go back to my condo because they're investigating still."

"You can just hide in the bathroom until I'm finished," Kat offered.

"No, I'm just going to get a room for tonight."

"Okay, I'll see you in the morning," Kat said while hugging her again. "Hold your head, Cherry."

"I will." She strolled to the front office to get a room.

When she approached the office, Jimmy, the hotel clerk jumped as if he saw a ghost. "Well, I'll be a monkey's uncle. Cherry! What you doing back here?"

"Hey, Jimmy." Chasity was almost embarrassed to be back at the Bay Shore Inn.

"Last thing I heard, you had given up the life, and you were living in a plush condo driving a BMW."

"Yeah, I left the life, and I had all that stuff, but I'm still not happy."

Jimmy saw the look of depression on her face. "Well, you look good."

"Thank you, Jimmy." She went inside her pockets. "Damn! I didn't bring any money." She was so fucked up that she forgot she left her house with nothing but the clothes she put on. "Jimmy, I'm sorry, but I didn't bring any money with me. But can I get a room for the night? I promise to pay you as soon as I get to my money tomorrow."

"Don't worry about it, baby. I can put you in one of these rooms free of charge. Hell, as much money as you spent here, we should give you a free room for a year."

"Thank you so much, Jimmy."

"Here. Room 216."

She took the key and went to her room and lay on the bed with the lights completely off. Images of Vinny, with blood squirting out of his neck, ran through her mind. She couldn't see Torian for some reason. Maybe it was because he was on the floor dead with no visible blood pouring out.

She thought about the time she spent with Torian. *He was so handsome, and his style was impeccable. I wish this had never happened. I wish I could close my eyes and wake up and this never happened.*

Her eyelids began to get heavy until they shut down. She'd been up for almost forty hours straight. Chasity fell into a dream state and skipped happily in a field of yellow daisies while wearing a white summer dress. On this bright summer day she was looking for someone.

"Torian! Where are you?" she asked. As she skipped through the field of daisies, she saw a huge tree. A man wearing immaculate white linen came into view.

"Torian? Is that you?"

He smiled. "Of course it's me, crazy ass girl! Come here!"

She ran toward him but moved in slow motion. Chasity couldn't reach him fast enough, so she started to look around nervously. When she finally reached him, his smile turned into a frown, and he hid behind the huge oak tree.

"Torian?" She stood waiting for him to reappear.

All around her, yellow daisies turned into red roses, and Vinny appeared instead of Torian. He was holding the same bouquet of roses he bought for her on their first meeting. Chasity's happy expression turned into a look of horror.

"Vinny? What the fuck are you doing here?"

"Oh, you're not happy to see me? I thought you loved me." Vinny scowled but also appeared confused.

"I did, but—"

"You don't have to lie anymore." He walked toward her. "I loved you!"

"No! Don't touch me!" She turned to run, but her legs moved in slow motion again.

She was running but Vinny walked casually and was still within arm's reach. He continued to stroll as she pumped her arms and legs with all her might.

"Come on legs! Go!" She finally realized she wasn't moving fast enough.

Vinny reached out for her. "Chasity! Grab my hand!"

"No!" She looked back to see his hand almost touch her shoulder. Her legs gained momentum, and she was now running fast enough to get away.

"Don't go!" Vinny yelled out.

She laughed as she increased her speed. "I'm out!"

Suddenly, the end of a high cliff came into view. She was moving too fast to slow down. "No!"

It was too late. Chasity tried to stop the momentum, but her sliding feet and flailing hands forced her off the cliff. She fell speedily; her heart beat hard and fast. It seemed as if an abyss awaited her at the end of her fall. The faster she descended, the harder and faster her heart pounded. She saw the ground coming up. *This is it*, she thought.

Chasity hit the ground with so much force it brought her back to the physical realm. She jumped up out of her slumber sweating and panting. Her heart beat at the same rate as it had in the dream. She took a few deep breaths to calm down. It took effect immediately. She sat up trying to make sense out of her dream which seemed like reality.

Alone and extremely frightened, she went to the bathroom and washed her face with cold water and looked at the reflection in the mirror. "What have I become?" Chasity tried to smile but she couldn't. Images from her dream broke her down, and she cried until she fell back to sleep.

This time there was no nightmares. But the nightmare wasn't over.

CHAPTER 10

The Money is Gone!

So you mean to tell me that there's no money in his account?" Jenny asked the bank teller. "My husband just deposited $3 million in this account eight months ago. Now he's dead and the money's gone!"

"Miss, there's nothing we can do about it. He withdrew all of the money in increments of $150 to $350,000 a month. Right up to . . ." The teller looked at his computer screen. "Last week was the last withdrawal."

There was a video recording of Vinny walking in the bank a week ago. The teller knew it was against the bank's policy, but he knew Jenny personally. He heard about the demise of her husband Vinny.

"I'm not supposed to show you this, so you didn't see it here. Understand?" He got up to close the door. "I'm going to show you who he came in here with. Maybe it'll help you get to your husband's money." He turned the screen toward her and played the footage of Vinny walking into the bank with Chasity on his arm. What hurt her was the happy expression on his face. *That fucking slut! I got something for her*, Jenny thought.

"I must admit, Vinny was acting strange on his last few visits to the bank," the bank teller announced.

"What do you mean?"

"Well, the way he was withdrawing his money triggered suspicion at the bank. So we're instructed to ask subtle questions just to ensure he wasn't being forced to withdraw the money. You know, like extortion or a kidnapping, that type of thing."

"Well, what did he say that triggered suspicion?" Jenny asked.

"When we asked him was there any reason he was taking such large chunks out of our bank, he replied that he was going away and he needed cash."

"That was all he said?"

"Oh yeah, he mentioned starting over, that's about it." Kevin knew this info was hurtful to Jenny, but he felt she needed to know.

"Thank you, Kevin. You don't know how much you've helped me today."

"Don't mention it, Jenny. I heard about what happened to Vinny. I'm sorry for your loss. I know you have the boys to take care of. Anything I can do to lighten the load."

"I really appreciate it," Jenny said with the utmost sincerity.

Jenny exited the bank and got into her Audi A8 and dialed a number. "Hey, cuz. I just left the bank. Just like we suspected, that fucking cunt knows something more than she was saying. She's been playing us the whole time."

"What do you mean she's been playing us the whole time? When I questioned her, she was candidly volunteering information."

"I just saw a video of her walking in and out of the bank with Vinny withdrawing $350,000! Did she tell you about that?" Jenny was almost screaming on the other end.

"Hmm. No, she didn't mention that. You're right. She played me."

"Where is she? Find her! This time I want that bitch tied up and tortured if she doesn't tell us where the money is! Even if I have to do it myself!" Jenny was fuming.

"Chill-out, Jenny. I got this. She left with Detective Samuels yesterday. He took her somewhere. It wasn't the condo, because it was still under investigation. She probably went to the Bay Shore Inn. She mentioned it in her interview."

"Let me know if you see her. I want to be there this time. This dumb cunt destroyed my family! I want revenge!" Jenny was seething with anger.

"I feel you, cuz, but we have to be smart. I already have my lieutenant suspicious of me. Any move we make has to be calculated. Let me handle it. I got you," Detective Colon replied sincerely.

Jenny was convinced that her big cousin had it all under control. "I know you got me, I'm just going through it right now. He left me with no money and two boys that need things—know what I'm saying?" Jenny sniffled.

"And to know that he was giving all of our money to some two-bit tramp! It just kills me, cuz."

"I know. She's going to get hers. Trust me. I got this. I owe it to the family to help you get Vinny's money back."

"I gotta go pick the boys up from school early. Since their father's death they've been given a pass to do a half day."

"How're they taking it?" Detective Colon asked.

"Hard." Jenny broke down. "Vinny Jr. said he wanted to kill himself, and Anthony just trashes his room every day, so I don't even bother fixing it up."

"Damn, cuz." Detective Colon was brought to tears. "Hold your head. I'll call you later with progress."

"Okay. Let me go get these boys. I'll talk to you later. Love you, big cuz."

"Love you too, lil cuz." Detective Colon hung up. *It's crazy. I watched her grow up. I remember when she was just a teenager, and now she's a mother of two and a widow.* She tuned out the busy everyday noises of the police department and sat at her desk taking it all in.

Detective Jennifer Colon was a fifteen year veteran of the Suffolk County Police Department's Narcotics Division. She was divorced five years now and had been single ever since. Most men couldn't handle her line of work. Her first cousin, who shared the same first name, Jennifer Vitaly was the wife of Vincent 'Vinny' Vitaly.

Jennifer was the name of their grandmother, the matriarch of the family. It was their family's tradition to name the girls Jennifer. There were a total of six females with the name Jennifer in their family.

Ironically, Detective Colon was born on the same day as her grandmother, Jennifer, and the younger Jennifer was born a day after their grandmother died. So they both shared a personal sentiment with the name Jennifer. That fact made them close. Detective Colon was seven years older, so she always treated Jenny like a little sister. Jenny was the only child, so she welcomed Detective Colon as an older sibling instead of an older cousin. Calling one another cuz was a childhood habit that stuck with them.

As Detective Colon sat at her cubicle thinking about Jenny. Detective Thomas strolled by.

"Excuse me, Detective Thomas. Can I have a word with you?" Detective Colon knew she had to be careful how she approached the conversation.

"Sure, champ," he replied sarcastically. "I saw your bout yesterday. You have some skills there, Colon."

"Thanks, Thomas." She blushed. "That's what I want to talk about. You don't know me for getting into any drama here at the department."

"I know. I was saying that to myself. You're the coolest female detective on the force. What happened?" Detective Thomas asked curiously.

"She was involved in a double murder. She was a witness. One of the men that was murdered was my brother-in-law."

"Wow, it's a small world. I didn't know what was going on." Detective Thomas was surprised.

"She got smart with her mouth, so I jumped across the table and clocked her in it." Colon didn't mention how she got a busted lip and a patch of hair missing.

"I wanted to let you guys get it off, but Detective Samuels came to her rescue." Thomas leaned in so he could whisper. "I think he's pumping her."

"Really?" Detective Colon knew there could be truth to his statement. "Why do you say that?"

"After he took her into his office I went to listen. I found it weird the way he picked her up and took her into his office."

"What did you hear?" Detective Colon already knew Thomas was eavesdropping on the conversation.

"I heard some talking, then I heard some moaning and shouting. *'I miss this so fucking much.'* It doesn't take a detective to figure out what that was."

"Interesting." She thought quickly. "How'd you like to make some money?"

"How much?" He smiled.

She smiled back. "At least six figures."

"Say no more." He wrote his cell phone number on a piece of paper. "This is my secure line. Call me on this line whenever you need me." He walked away.

Detective Colon picked up the paper and put the number in her phone. "I'm going to find you, and when I do it's not going to be good for you." She looked at the Facebook pics of Chasity with venom in her blood.

CHAPTER 11

Now You Know!

"What the fuck does that shit mean?" she asked herself as she lay in the bed. The image that kept occurring was the one of Torian wearing all white standing by a huge oak tree. The vision stayed stuck in her mind. Even when she tried to think of something else, she couldn't get it out.

"A tree, what does a tree have to do with anything?" she asked herself, trying to make sense out of the dream sequence.

The ringing phone brought her out of her session. She looked at the caller ID. It was Kat.

"What's up, thot?" Chasity said with a throat full of gravel from just waking up.

"You tell me, thot. I got a fat blunt already rolled and ready to smoke."

"I'll be there in five minutes."

Chasity jumped up and took a piss. Then she brushed her teeth and washed her face. She threw on some Marc Jacobs sweat pants and a sweat shirt. She was at Kat's door in less than five minutes.

Knock, knock!

Kat came to the door. "You wasn't lying when you said you'll be here in five minutes."

"I'm trying to smoke to get my mind off of this dream!" Chasity declared. "I had this fucked up dream last night."

"What was it about?"

Chasity started shaking her head. "At first it was pleasant. I was running through a field of yellow daisies. Then I saw a tree, and Torian was standing there smiling. I approached him and he got sad and hid from me." She paused to spark the blunt. "That's when Vinny appeared with red roses. The same red roses he used to bring me when we first met. Then the yellow daisies turned into the red roses. I started running from Vinny, and he was trying to stop me, trying to warn me, but I kept running from him and fell off a deep cliff. That's when I woke up."

"That shit sounds deep, my nigga," Kat responded while taking a pull of the blunt.

"When I woke up, all I could see was Torian standing by this huge oak tree wearing all white, smiling . . ." She inhaled the blunt, then passed it to Kat.

"That shit be meaning something, my G. Every dream has a secret meaning. You just have to figure it out." Kat exhaled a thick cloud of smoke.

"I know. I'm trying to make sense out of it, but everything is crazy in my head right now. This shit just happened yesterday. This nigga ain't even fresh in the ground yet. That's what makes the dream so scary." Chasity got goose bumps thinking about Torian.

"What are you going to do now?" Kat asked. "You still have the BMW and the condo, and some money, I hope." Chasity told Kat about the money.

"Yeah, I have the BMW, but I'm not staying in that condo. I witnessed that whole shit go down. That place is haunted. You can have it if you want."

"Are you serious? I can have that fly ass condo?" Kat asked in disbelief.

"If you want it. I'm not visiting you if you stay there." Chasity was adamant about not going back to the condo.

Kat's silence spoke her heart, but Chasity's state of mind overlooked it. They finished smoking the blunt. Kat had some Henny sitting on the dresser. Chasity saw it and quickly grabbed it. She gulped down a hefty portion.

"Damn, thot! You must've been thirsty. Drinking my Henny like that," Kat protested.

"Shut up, thot! As much Henny as I bought for your broke ass!" Chasity responded playfully.

"Broke ass? Thot, if it wasn't for your deceased sugar daddy, you would be broke just like me! Don't try to front up in here!" Kat's tone was offensive.

"What you sayin'?" Chasity noticed her tone. "You do the same thing as me. Don't hate 'cause don't no baller want to sweep you off your raggedy feet!"

"I had plenty of niggas that wanted to wife me, boo-boo!"

"Where they at?" Chasity looked around the room. "Exactly!"

Kat couldn't come up with a comeback fast enough. "Look, I got better things to do. I have to get ready for my trap." She opened her room door.

"Oh, it's like that. You kicking me out because you want to start some shit that you can't handle. I see how you really are." Chasity started walking out of the room. "I'll give my condo to someone that'll appreciate it."

"You can keep that shit!" Kat slammed the door on Chasity's back.

******

Detective Colon sat in the parking lot of the Bay Shore Inn waiting to see if Chasity would appear. She had been sitting there for the last thirty minutes that Chasity was in Kat's room. When the door to Kat's room opened, she saw Chasity exit.

"There she goes! Let's see what room she goes to." Chasity walked down to room 216. Detective Colon wrote it down on a piece of paper. "Got you now, cunt!" She cocked back her police issued 9-millimeter Glock.

Detective Colon was just about to get out and knock on the door when she saw Detective Samuels pull up and park. He pulled his cell phone out as if to make a call.

"Thousand dollars says he's calling Chasity," she said to herself.

Two minutes later, he got out of his car and headed toward room 216.

"Detective Samuels to the rescue once again," Colon said, easing down in her seat to stay as incognito as possible.

******

"Thanks for checking up on me," Chasity said as she opened the door to let Detective Samuels in.

"No problem." He kissed her on the cheek. "I really came by to give you some information."

"Some information? What information?" Chasity asked.

"It seems that someone was contacting Mr. Vitaly, which was against your better interest."

"What do you mean 'against my better interest'? Speak in regular terms, Tommy."

"Well, we checked Mr. Vitaly's text messages—"

"You mean Vinny?" Chasity wasn't used to Vinny being referred to as Mr. Vitaly.

"Yes, Vinny. We checked his messages, and we saw a series of messages with someone that he didn't store in his phone. And it's a throw-away phone, so we can't trace the name of the owner." Detective Samuels handed her some paper. "Here is a readout of the messages."

Chasity read the messages. There was just a phone number for the identity of the mystery person. She looked at the number. "This number looks so familiar to me. But I smoke so much weed, and who memorizes phone numbers anymore?"

"Read the messages, and maybe you'll get a hint of who is writing them," Detective Samuels suggested.

"Okay." Chasity began reading the messages.

MESSAGE #1

631-223-4477: *Hey!*

Vinny: *Who's this?*

631-223-4477: *A secret admirer.*

Vinny: *Stop playing around. Who is this?*

631-223-4477: *I know that Cherry isn't being honest with U. When U R ready 4 a real woman 2 treat U good, call me.*

Vinny: *How do you know Cherry isn't treating me right?*

631-223-4477: *Keep this between me and U and I'll keep U posted.*

MESSAGE #2

631-223-4477: *Ask her about Torian*

Vinny: *Who is Torian?*

631-223-4477: *That's Cherry's other man. The one she's with when U R not around. I know she told U she's only with U, but she's lying.*

Chasity gasped. "I remember when he asked me about Torian. I kept trying to figure out how he knew his name! Now I know," Chasity said aloud.

MESSAGE #3

631-223-4477: *She promised she wouldn't have any man in the condo U bought 4 her*

Vinny: *I'm out of town. How would I know you're telling the truth?*

631-223-4477: *When U come back schedule another trip. But go & see 4 yourself if she won't have Torian all up in that condo. When you catch her I want 2 be your new woman. I can please U better than she can & I'll be loyal.*

Vinny: *Let me get a sample since you bragging.*

631-223-4477: *Come 2 the Bay Shore Inn. Room 220. I'll take U on a ride around the world!*

"Wait a minute!" Chasity looked at the number again. "Bay Shore Inn? There's only one person that is always up in the Bay Shore Inn and that's Kat's nasty ass!"

She tried to put the number in her phone, but she couldn't see the screen because it was cracked. "I can't see my screen, but I'm willing to bet a million dollars that this number belongs to Kat!"

Chasity kept reading the messages. There was one last group of messages, and they were dated yesterday. Right before Vinny was murdered.

631-223-4477: *They're on their way 2 the condo as we speak.*

Vinny: *You sure?*

631-223-4477: *They just left me & they're headed 4 the condo. If U get there B4 them U can hide in the closet & catch her in the act so she can't lie.*

Vinny: *If you're right & I catch her in the act you'll be rewarded as my next lady.*

631-223-4477: *Really daddy! So U did like my special treatment?*

Vinny: *Like it, I loved it!*

631-223-4477: *Ok daddy. Hurry up so U can catch them*

Vinny: *Ok*

That was the last text that Vinny would make in this lifetime.

"That sneaky, no good slut!" Chasity was so angry she almost ran over to Kat's room to pummel her. "That's why she was coming at me like that today."

"The best thing to do is lay low and let this thing die down. There's still the issue of Detective Colon. Something still doesn't sit right with me about that."

Chasity was still thinking about what Kat did. She had to go back into time and try to drum up the memory. "The last person I spoke to about my personal business was Kat. She was playing me the whole time," Chasity recalled.

"What do you mean? Explain."

"Kat was my confidant. I told her everything. She knew that Vinny didn't want me to be with anyone but him. She also knew that I was still fucking around with Torian. I'm convinced she told Vinny that me and Torian were on our way to the condo." Chasity was hurt by Kat's betrayal.

"Now you know. Play her to your advantage. You can use her if need be. If not, throw her to the wolves," Detective Samuels said while looking at his watch. "I have to go to work."

"Do me a favor and drop me off at my condo so I can get the keys to my car and a change of clothes."

"No problem."

*****

As they exited the room, Detective Colon watched. They both got into Detective Samuels' vehicle. Detective Colon followed them directly to Chasity's condo. When they got to the gate, Chasity got out and identified herself to the guard. In turn, he let them into the gated community.

Detective Colon couldn't get in without permission. She didn't want to blow her cover, so she just parked outside the gate and waited. Ten minutes later, Detective Samuels drove out with an empty passenger seat.

She viewed her watch. "I remember her saying she drives a black BMW. I'll sit here for one hour, then I have to go." Detective Colon sat in the car playing Candy Crush on her phone, waiting on her prey.

Patiently waiting.

CHAPTER 12

Now That's What I Call Magic!

BAY SHORE INN

This one's for you, my nigga." Sincere's eyes began to water. Kat and Sincere sat in her room smoking a blunt of his finest weed. Sincere inhaled the smoke and choked as he exhaled.

"Word," Kat added. "Torian was a fly dude. Fucking with the wrong bitch will get you killed."

"I hate that bitch Cherry for what she did to my man. She knew that white boy was crazy. She could've did her dirt elsewhere. How that nigga found out she had Torian up in the crib is a mystery." Sincere wiped the tears that were now falling.

Kat didn't speak. She knew the culprit that Sincere was speaking of. She had told Vinny that Chasity was headed to the condo with Torian that day. *I didn't think he had it in him to kill the nigga. I wouldn't have told him if I would've known he'd do this shit*, Kat thought.

"I'll be right back." Kat got up to go to the bathroom, knowing Sincere was watching her big ass as it swayed back and forth like a pendulum.

She returned a moment later and sat down close to Sincere. "I'm saying though. Let me get that ounce."

"What you got for me?" Sincere rubbed his hands up and down her thick thighs. "You thicker than a Snicker up in this bitch!"

"You like it?" Kat stood up and made her ass clap. "Go ahead and touch it. Don't be scared."

Sincere palmed her ass. "And that shit soft as cotton too!" He stood up and unzipped his pants and took his penis out. "Let me see what that mouth do."

Kat went down on him as if she was moving in slow motion. She stared at him with a seductive expression so intense, Sincere almost lost his concentration. Kat knew Sincere was fucking Chasity, so she had to go into her bag of tricks to top her. *I'm going to fuck the shit out of this nigga.*

She sucked soft and slow, and then she built up into a sucking frenzy. "Damn, ma! You got skills for real!" Sincere's toes were trying to curl, but he was standing, which prevented them from doing so.

"Umm hmm, you slept on me for the red bone bitch!" She sucked him harder.

"Never again! I promise you that! Oh shit, I'm about to come!" Sincere couldn't hold it back.

Kat stopped and squeezed his dick. "No! I don't want you to come yet!" She squeezed until she felt the swelling go down.

"How you going to do that? I was about to bust a load right in that mouth!"

That's when she took a condom out of the dresser and put it in her mouth. Then she put his dick in her mouth. Once it came out, the condom was on it.

"Now that's what I call magic!" Sincere declared.

She stood and pulled her spandex off, and her big, round ass spread out like a blanket. It was bigger and rounder when she bent over.

"Damn that shit look pretty!" he said.

Sincere got behind her and inserted his penis into her love tunnel. "Oh yeah! Fuck that pussy!" Kat egged him on. Sincere pumped in and out until he ejaculated and fell out on the bed. "That was some good fucking pussy! If I would've known it was like that, I would've hit that shit a long time ago."

Kat let him rest, but she had other things on her mind. After fifteen minutes, she was ready to lay down her plan.

"You know that was really fucked up how Cherry got Torian killed like that."

"Yeah, it was," Sincere added.

"She should get hers. She think she all that. I should get her robbed. I know about all the money she got from Vinny." Kat threw out the bait.

"Money, what money?" Just that quick, Sincere took the bait.

"That nigga gave her $350,000. Then he was taking money out and just splurging on her like she was the first lady or some fucking body. So she wasn't even spending the money he gave her. She should at least have $300,000 left."

Sincere always squinted his eyes and rubbed his chin when he was deep in thought. "So, you know this is a fact?"

"Facts, my G! She used to tell me everything when she was my homie. But she played herself and tried to get fly and she got swatted."

The truth was, Kat became extremely jealous of Chasity after she'd met Vinny. Before Vinny, they were both financially equal. Afterward, Chasity left Kat in the dust. There was no way for Kat to compete, unless she hit the lottery. Chasity had a way of flaunting her newfound wealth, which added insult to injury. That's why Kat stole Vinny's number from her phone, in an attempt to live the life Chasity was living. But it backfired! Now no one was getting any money.

"Do you know where she's at?" Sincere asked.

"She's in room 216. We can tie that bitch up and torture her. I bet she'll give up that money then," Kat suggested.

"That sounds like a plan." Sincere thought about Torian. "I'm doing it for you, Torian." Although Sincere made the declaration, it was really about him coming up.

"I'm going to make friends with her, and that's when I'm going to call you to come through, and we can do it right here," Kat offered.

"Okay, just let me know. I'm definitely with it. Then we can keep this going."

"Let me get an ounce," Kat asked before Sincere was about to step out.

"I got you next time." He swiftly left the room so she couldn't protest. *Fuck that thot! I ain't giving her shit! But hard dick and a Happy Meal!* Sincere laughed.

"Wait!" Kat got up to give chase, but it was too late. Sincere was out the door and in his car. "Sincere is a foul ass dude!" She picked up the small left over blunt and tried to get a few pulls out of it. "I don't even know if I should trust his ass."

******

Detective Colon was about to pull off when Chasity pulled up to the gate. "There she goes!"

The detective started her vehicle and got in a position to follow Chasity. Chasity didn't notice Detective Colon tailing her, but she drove like she knew. She'd gone from zero to sixty in four seconds, leaving Detective Colon six cars behind. There was no way for her to keep up with the speed of the BMW.

"Slow down, you fucking cunt!" Detective Colon raved. "Where's the fucking cops when you need them?"

She drove looking at every car, hoping that she'd caught up to Chasity, but she didn't. She lost her.

"Fuck! This bitch keeps slipping through my fingers. But when I do get my hands on you, I'm going to squeeze the life out of you."

******

With visions of wringing Kat's neck, Chasity drove fast with the radio blasting as usual. She pulled into the storage facility and put her code in and the gates lifted. She drove directly to the storage unit marked 70B and parked. Chasity got out and opened the unit with a key, and then closed it behind her. There was a safe on the floor. She put in the combination and opened it.

There was a total of $1.7 million in cash, all in ten thousand dollar stacks. "It's all here. Now I have to get this shit out of here without anyone knowing." She knew she had to be very discreet about her knowledge of Vinny's money. Vinny warned her on many occasions that Rocco and his cohorts wanted to get their hands on it, but they didn't know where Vinny was hiding the money. They weren't the only people who wanted to get their hands on the mountain of cash. Detective Colon was on Chasity's trail. It was only a matter of time before they collided.

"How did I even get myself in this situation in the first place?" Chasity asked herself. She looked at all the money and thought back.

CHAPTER 13

IF IT AINT ABOUT THE MONEY!

Six months ago . . .

Listen, Vinny, the family is worried about how you're spending all your money on this fucking chick!" Rocco said furiously. "Enough is enough! You got the whole family looking like jerk-offs! Everyone sees you out with this broad. Jenny knows about it. The whole fucking family knows about it!"

Vinny smiled as Rocco screamed. Rocco was a little older that Vinny, so he felt he had the authority to raise his voice to him. What Rocco didn't understand was that yelling only made Vinny more rebellious. They weren't kids anymore.

"What the fuck are you smiling about? I'm dead fucking serious, and you're fucking smiling!" Rocco took that as disrespect.

"I hear what you're saying. But why does anybody really care how I'm spending my money. It's my hard earned money. I deserve the right to spend it how I please. Just because she's black, or she used to be a prostitute, doesn't give anyone the right to judge." Vinny spoke calmly. So calm that it disturbed Rocco.

"Are you okay, Vinny?" Rocco stared into his eyes. They were glassy. "You seem a little off or something."

"I'm fine, couldn't feel any better." Vinny's response was cool and measured.

"I hope you at least pay attention to some of what I told you. That chick is bad news. I can smell it. But to each his own. If you want to lay in the dirt, fine. But you won't tarnish the reputation of this family." Rocco stormed off.

Vinny smiled as if Rocco had just told him a pleasant joke. He looked at his Rolex sky dweller. "About that time."

He waltzed to his Range Rover and sat in the driver's seat. He looked at his reflection in the rearview mirror. Then he looked at the glove compartment and opened it. The bottle of prescription pills inside read: Oxycodone. He opened it, took out a pill and looked at it. He tossed it in his mouth, and then he put another one in his hand. *Should I take two?* he thought. *Fuck it!* He threw the other pill in his mouth and closed the bottle.

Fifteen minutes later, he was smiling cheek to cheek. "I think I'm going to take out another $300,000 tomorrow." Vinny grinned as he spoke to himself. "Yeah, that's what I'll do." The powerful substance took him to another place.

About a year ago, Vinny had a back injury from improperly lifting a stack of two by fours off a truck. It got so bad his doctor prescribed Oxycodone for the pain. Vinny popped them at will, getting his prescription filled quicker than the previous. In a matter of two months,

Vinny was addicted to prescription drugs. Spending anywhere from $1,500 to $3,000 a month on prescription drugs.

Taking the drugs altered his personality. Normally he wasn't a big gambler. He liked to play an occasional game of poker with the boys every now and then. Now he was blowing money fast on the horses and at the poker table every week at different casinos. There was no limit to how much he'd blow in a night. When he wasn't blowing money at the casino, he was blowing it on Chasity, who became the envy of the town.

Chasity wore an iced-out female Rolex with a matching Rolex pinky ring. A twenty-five karat diamond tennis bracelet with five karats in each ear. Vinny brought her a full-length sable. He spent over $350,000 on her, which was what he initially gave her.

"Babe, I need you to come with me to the bank today," Vinny said. "It's important."

"Okay, just let me get dressed, and I'll go with you to the bank." Chasity always liked going where the money was.

She dressed in a beautiful white silk blouse with a red silk skirt that showed off her voluptuous curves, and red and white Christian Louboutin high heels. "How do I look, baby?" she asked Vinny, knowing she looked stunning.

"You look absolutely gorgeous, honey." Vinny kissed her on the cheek. "That's why I love you so much."

They drove in Vinny's Range Rover. Neither one of them noticed the black Lincoln MKZ with tinted windows following them.

******

"What can we do for you today?" Kevin asked Vinny, while trying to keep his eyes away from Chasity's cleavage.

"I want to take out another $300,000," Vinny said.

"Is there a reason why you're taking so much money out of our bank, Mr. Vitaly?" Kevin asked with a stone face.

Vinny glanced at Chasity. "I thought it was a free country," he answered sarcastically.

"No, we have to ask those types of questions just in case you're being forced to take out money against your will," Kevin answered nervously.

"I'm thinking about moving away, and I need all the cash I can get." Vinny's answer didn't put Kevin at ease, but it raised the red flag higher.

"Okay, Mr. Vitaly, how would you like that $300,000?"

"In stacks of $10,000. And give me one of those complementary briefcases to walk out of here with."

"Not a problem, sir." Kevin dashed to the back of the bank.

Fifteen minutes later, Kevin came back with a black briefcase, and he opened it. "It's all there just like you wanted it. In increments of $10,000."

Vinny looked at the crisp money. He grabbed a stack and flipped through it. "Good old fashion moolah." Then he closed it. "Always a pleasure doing business with you."

Vinny and Chasity walked out of Chase bank with every male employee trying to get one last look at Chasity's back side before she was gone.

"That sure wasn't Mrs. Vitaly," Kevin said to his co-worker.

"That's for sure," his co-worker responded.

******

Rocco followed them to Chase bank and parked out of view. He watched the two of them walk into the bank hand in hand as if they were married. He admired Chasity.

"She is a looker! She's fucking gorgeous just like Vinny said." Rocco was in awe of Chasity's beauty. "I'd love to fuck the shit out of all her holes." Rocco sat in his car lusting and waiting for them to come out.

Tthe briefcase in Vinny's hand caught Rocco's attention as he walked out of the bank with Chasity. He knew when he entered the bank he wasn't carrying anything. So he surmised that there was money in the briefcase.

"Let's see where you and your lady are taking this money."

He trailed them to a storage unit, but he wasn't able to get in because he didn't know the code. He was stuck on the other side. Rocco needed to see exactly which storage unit they were going to.

"Fuck!" Rocco cursed himself. "At least I know what storage facility he's using." Rocco made a mental note of the address and drove away. He'd seen enough.

******

Vinny drove to storage unit 70B and parked.

"Listen, there's something I have to tell you." Vinny became serious.

"What is it, babe?" Chasity was nervous, so she secretly placed her hand in her purse and gripped her .25 caliber automatic.

"We might have to get out of town on a moment's notice one day. I need you to know where I stash my cash just in case something happens to me." Vinny made sure she was paying close attention.

"You're scaring me, babe. Why would we have to just leave on a moment's notice? What's really going on, Vinny?" He got out of the car and opened the storage gate. "Come on, I have to show you something."

Chasity got out slowly with one hand in her purse, clutching her weapon. *You never know about these crazy ass white people*, she thought and followed him into the storage. He closed the gate and turned on the light.

"My family doesn't approve of us, and they're threatening to cut me off. So I just feel like if they ever try anything, I'll be prepared. That's why I've been taking all my money out of the bank and storing it here." He pointed toward the safe. "Here's the combination and the key to the storage. There's only two copies of the key, so guard it with your life." He handed her a key and a small piece of paper that read: Left 24, Right 36, Left 39. "See if you can open it."

Chasity read the instructions and the safe was opened. When she saw all the cold cash piled up in the safe she almost had an orgasm. "I've never seen this much money before in my life!" she said in amazement.

Vinny took the money out of the briefcase and neatly stacked it with the other money in the safe. Before closing it, he grabbed six $10,000 stacks, and he handed Chasity two.

"Go buy yourself something nice."

"I sure will," she declared.

"Now, let's go to Atlantic City for the weekend!"

"Atlantic City," she whispered. "I remember the last time I was in Atlantic City."

"What you say, babe?"

"Nothing, I was just thinking about the last time I was in Atlantic City." *Torian!* She got moist.

They went to Atlantic City, and the whole time she thought about Torian. Everything about Atlantic City screened images of the time she spent there with him. She couldn't wait to get back to New York to quench the burning desire to speak to Torian, to be with him. She couldn't resist the urge to reach out to him.

Chasity was living the life of her dreams. She ate out at restaurants three times a day. Did whatever she desired every day without thinking about the cost. She did everything she wanted to do but one thing—be with Torian.

Even though she was hurt when she found out he had a wife and two sons, she couldn't get him out of her mind. She knew if he came back into her life she would take him. It had been almost two months since the fiasco with his baby's mother, Tondra. Torian made a few attempts at calling her to no avail. So he gave up. He wasn't one for sweating any chick.

Chasity missed Torian so much she wrestled with the thoughts of calling him every day. She grew tiresome of pretending to like Vinny, and going with him on gambling trips. She wanted to spend time with someone who was on her level of vibe. Vinny just wasn't it, no matter how hard he tried. Chasity would never submit to really loving him.

"You know what? Fuck it! I'm going to call him today." Chasity dialed his number, and he answered on the second ring.

"What's shaking, Cherry?" Torian said solemnly. "I didn't think I was going to ever hear from you again."

"You weren't, but I got over it and I actually missed you." Chasity smiled.

"You missed me? I don't believe that. It's been almost two months since that incident."

"You lucky I'm calling at all," she said sternly. "Because no nigga has ever played me like that before, and they won't ever again!"

"You right. You don't deserve that. I'm sorry for lying to you. I just thought you wouldn't fuck with me if I told you the truth."

"You can always tell me the truth, Torian. That's all I ask. I don't need any money, or anything. All I need is honesty, trust." She spoke from the heart.

"I can give it to you, Cherry. I did miss the hell out of you," Torian responded sincerely.

"Are you still with your baby mother?" Chasity almost held her breath.

"No, she really left me this time. It wasn't the first time I got caught cheating," Torian admitted.

Chasity let out a sigh of relief when Torian told her he was single now. *Yes! Thank you Lord!*

"What are you doing tonight?" Chasity asked.

"Nothing, I was about to go to the gym when you called. After that I was just going to go to Sincere's to kick it a minute," Torian answered.

"Fuck that nigga Sincere. Come and see me after the gym."

"How about I skip the gym and come and work you out?"

Chasity's vagina spasmed when he said those words.

"Meet me at the Hyatt on Wicks Road in an hour." She hung up.

Those memories made her heart patter. She felt a ping of pure sadness knowing she would never see or feel his touch again. What killed her most of all was the thought that this all could've been avoided if she did things different.

"If only I would've left him alone after I caught him lying. He would still be alive. If I would've kept it official with Vinny and just told him that I was fucking with another guy but for him to just accept it."

She looked at all the money. It amazed her now just like it did the first time Vinny brought her here and gave her the key and combination to the safe. She kept staring at all the money, and then she thought about how much grief it caused. How it caused people to cross one another and kill just to possess it. The amazement turned to shame and disgust.

"All for the love of money." She wiped the tears with the back of her hand.

Chasity took out five $10,000 stacks and pulled down the gate. When she got in the car and turned the radio on, the appropriate song was playing. The lyrics fit perfectly with what was going on in her life at the present moment.

"If it ain't about the money/don't be blowing me up if I ain't getting none/Bitch you can miss me with it/bitch nigga miss me wit it/Turn up!" Chasity sang along to TI's hit song, "If It Ain't About the Money." She sped on the Long Island Expressway headed nowhere fast. Singing along to the soundtrack of her life.

CHAPTER 14

I Hope You Can Forgive Me

"What do you mean you can't find her?" Jenny asked Detective Colon. "You're a fucking detective!"

"Watch your fucking tone!" Detective Colon quickly checked her little cousin. "I was following her and she was speeding in her BMW and I lost her," Detective Colon explained.

"We have to find her because my children are about to go starving if I don't get that money fast!" Jenny was being a bitch by laying the guilt trip on her older cousin.

"I'm on it. I know a way to track her. I just need her cell phone number. I didn't want to ask Detective Samuels. He's in charge of the case now. I know he's on her side."

"All you need is her phone number!" Jenny smiled from ear to ear, "Why didn't you just ask? I have her cell phone number. I took it out of Vinny's phone while he was sleeping here one night."

"Great! With her cell phone I can turn on her GPS and track her down as long as she has the phone on her." Detective Colon was excited too. "Text me the number. I'll have her location in a matter of minutes!"

Jenny texted Detective Colon Chasity's cell phone number. Just like she said, it only took her ten minutes to use the GPS app that only detectives had. It tracked

Chasity down to her exact location. She looked at her cell phone screen. There was a red circle indicating Chasity's location.

"There she is!" Detective Colon's face lit up. "This says she's at Red Lobster. Enjoy the meal, because it may be your last." Detective Colon put on her siren and sped toward Red Lobster.

******

"Is it just you today? Or will you be expecting someone?" the waitress asked Chasity while smiling.

"Yes, I'm expecting someone."

"Okay, come this way." The waitress led her to a cozy booth. "Is a booth okay?"

"Yes, that's fine." Chasity sat in the booth. "Can you bring me a long island ice tea please?"

"Sure. I'll be right back with your drink." She scurried away.

I wish I could smoke a fat blunt right here, right now, Chasity thought. She didn't have a weed connect to buy from, and she felt funny about calling Sincere, knowing that he and Torian were best friends. She would ask Kat, but she was done with her after finding out that she may be the one who told Vinny about Torian.

"I guess I have to go cold turkey." As she spoke, her long island ice tea was served. "I guess I have to just drink it down for now." She drank half of the tall glass of strong alcoholic drink.

Two more gulps and she was feeling it. "Where's this nigga Tommy at? He was supposed to beat me here."

She looked at her Rolex. It was 6:30 p.m.

******

Detective Colon pulled up to Red Lobster and looked at her watch. "Six-thirty. She shouldn't be in here any longer than two hours." She took a deep breath and fidgeted with her service weapon, "You have to come up for air sooner or later."

She sat in her unmarked police vehicle and waited. Five minutes later she saw Detective Samuels pull up. "What the fuck are you doing here, Samuels?" she asked herself furiously.

He parked his vehicle and dashed to the entrance. He didn't see Detective Colon, but he looked straight in her direction. She almost panicked until she realized the front window was tinted as well.

"Fucking Captain Save-a-Ho to the rescue." She knew he was there to see Chasity.

She waited.

******

Chasity looked at her watch. "Six-thirty-five. I'm ready to get out of here." She gulped down the rest of her drink and stood up to leave when she saw Detective Samuels checking in with the waitress.

The waitress guided him to Chasity's booth. "I was about to leave! You said you'd be here at six on the dot!"

"Sorry about that. I had to take care of some police business." He sat down across from Chasity and stared at her for ten seconds. *Damn, she is fucking gorgeous!*

"Why the fuck are you staring at me like that, Tommy?" He had a creepy look on his face.

"Excuse me. I was just admiring your beauty. You look rather ravishing today, Cherry."

"Thanks, Tommy. I don't feel ravishing, but thanks anyway."

"Listen, you were right about the phone number." He handed her four black and white photos. "Is this your friend Kat?"

She looked at the photos with disgust. "Yeah, that's the sneaky ass bitch." Chasity thought Kat was her BFF. So she was hurt and mad at the same time.

"Does she have any motive to do you harm? Did you guys have a fall out or something?" Detective Samuels asked.

"It was all good until I met Vinny and started living the life. She wanted to be me, to live like me, so she did some grease ball shit. A classic case of playa hating."

"I see." Detective Samuels thought about the new info. "This could be more serious than you think. Most murders are done by someone close, and the number one motivation is money, hate, or jealousy. Don't take it too lightly, she could've killed you."

Chasity thought about her past dealings with Kat. *Did I tell her about the money?*

"Girl I got Vinny so open. This nigga hit a lick at his construction company for $30 million, so he broke me off with a cool $350,000. Top notch pimping! Know what I'm saying?"

"Damn! You serious? This nigga gave you $350,000!" Kat was perplexed. *"Open up your legs."*

"For what?" Chasity asked curiously.

"So I can see what the fuck you got up in that pussy of yours that got this dude going hard like that!"

Chasity laughed. "You stupid, Kat!" She was actually flattered.

"I'm trying to come up like that one day." Kat suddenly wore a devilish grin.

Chasity got a glimpse of the expression on Kat's face but paid it no mind.

"That's why that bitch had that sneaky ass grin on her face the day I told her!" Chasity said out loud.

Detective Samuels sat quietly while Chasity was in thought. "She had a sneaky ass grin on her face the day you told her what?" he asked, trying to put the pieces of the puzzle together.

Chasity was hesitant. ". . . When I told her about the money that Vinny gave me."

"How much money we talking about? A couple hundred, or a couple of thousand?"

"Three hundred fifty thousand dollars."

His expression went from calm to surprised. "Three hundred fifty thousand dollars! He gave you $350,000 in exchange for what?"

"In exchange for me to be his mistress, his sex slave. I accepted the money and that's how I ended up in this whole mess."

"This is far more serious than I thought. If you told Kat, and we know for sure she was the one who told Vinny—there is a clear motive for anyone to make you a target."

"Why do you say anyone?"

"You don't know who she told, or who she's conspiring with. And I still need to know why Detective Colon was so invested in you. She almost lost her job with that little act the other day. Now that you tell me there's that amount of money involved, I'll bet money was her motivation as well."

Chasity thought about what he said. "You're right, because she was throwing me hate from the gate. I was so out of it from witnessing the murders that I didn't peep it at first. But now that we're speaking about it, she definitely had a serious grudge against me."

"I'm going to look into her when I get back to the station." He glanced at his watch. "I have to get back to work. Will I see you later?" Detective Samuels was fiending for her.

"Call me." She stood to give him a hug and a kiss on the cheek. "I'm out of here too. I just lost my appetite."

"I'll cover the check," Detective Samuels offered.

They both walked out, but not together. Detective Samuels went his way and Chasity went her way.

"Hey Cherry!" Samuels yelled.

She looked back in acknowledgement without speaking.

"Watch your back and be on point."

******

"That's it, go your separate ways," Detective Colon said as Chasity got into her BMW and headed west on Sunrise Highway. She didn't need to speed, so she calmly started her car and followed the red circle on her screen.

"Piece of cake. You're not getting away this time," Detective Colon said as followed the red dot.

CHAPTER 15

It's All About the Money

This is what I'm going to do," Sincere said to Kat. "I'm going to call her and make her feel at ease about the whole situation. Know what I mean?"

"Yeah, just be real smooth. You know she'll do anything for the weed you got," Kat replied.

Sincere called Chasity's number.

Reluctantly she answered, "Hello?"

"What's up, Cherry? How you been?" Sincere faked concern.

"Not too well, how about you?"

"I'm fucked up over that shit! That was my best friend since first grade. My A-1 since day one."

"I know, he felt the same about you." Chasity felt the lumps swelling up in her throat.

"I know you were starting to love Torian, and he was feeling the same way about you. I just wanted to reach out because I know you think I blame you for what happened, but I don't. Everything happens for a reason. It's not your fault."

Chasity let out a loud sigh. "Thank you so much, Sincere. That means the world to me because I thought you hated me. I know how it looks, that's why I was hesitant to call you. Lord knows I need that medicine."

"I got you! Where you at? I'll meet up with you. I got some fire too!" Sincere knew the weed was the ultimate lure for Chasity.

"I'm on Sunrise Highway headed west. Do you want to meet at Timberline Park?"

"Yeah, we can meet there. How long?" Sincere glanced at Kat and winked.

"I can be there in ten minutes."

"Okay, I'll see you there." Sincere hung up. "You got the rope and the duct tape?" he asked Kat.

"Yep! It's all right here." She opened her big purse, revealing the items he asked her to get.

"Cool. This is the plan. When she pulls up, I'm going to get out to serve her. I'm going to ask her to get out of the car for a hug. That's when you come from behind and hit her in the head and throw her into my trunk. We can take her to this abandoned warehouse. It's a remote spot in the woods, so no one should be coming through there."

"Sounds like a plan," Kat agreed.

"Let's make it to Timberline before she gets there."

******

Chasity felt a release of pressure talking to Sincere. She knew he had every right to hate her for how Torian got murdered. She couldn't wait to meet up with Sincere to get her medicine. She was a chronic smoker, so any amount of time not high caused her some anxiety.

When she pulled up near Sincere's blue Lexus, she parked next to him and got out.

Sincere got out to greet her. "Hey, pretty girl!" He held his arms out for a hug.

Chasity embraced him. He squeezed her extra tight and long. "Okay, you can let go now!" she protested, feeling the pressure of his arms wrapped around her. Instead of releasing her, he lengthened his embrace and increased his grasp. "Stop! You're hurting me!"

Kat came from out of the bushes with a Billy club and hit her in the back of her head so hard Sincere felt it. Chasity was out instantly. Sincere opened his trunk and tossed her limp body inside. Kat quickly tied her hands up with the rope and duct taped her mouth. He jumped in the car with Kat in the passenger side and sped off.

Chasity left her car running with her cell phone plugged up to the charger.

******

"Timberline Park, my old stomping grounds. I wonder what she's up to."

As Detective Colon was pulling into the entrance of Timberline Park, she saw a blue Lexus speeding on its way out. "Slow down, asshole!" she shouted. "Lucky there's no kids out here at this time."

She made a mental note of the make and model of the car just as a force of police work habit. She followed the red dot to its location. Chasity's black BMW sat parked, but there was no sign of Chasity. She looked around the park. There was no one there. Just the parked BMW.

"That's strange." She drove up to the BMW and got out and looked around it. It was still running. She opened the door. Chasity's cell phone was sitting in the middle console.

"Fuck! She's not here!"

Frantically she looked around the park, then she quickly thought about the blue Lexus speeding out of the park as she entered. She took the keys out of the BMW and jumped in her vehicle and turned on her siren. "The blue Lexus! She's in the blue Lexus!"

Detective Colon sped toward the direction of the Lexus.

******

"That looks like the dicks coming in," Kat said, noticing Detective Colon's car entering the park as they were exiting.

"You right! Fuck!" Sincere pressed the gas and looked in the rearview. "He's not coming after me, but I'm out. That was a close call." He drove as fast as possible toward the location. The coast was clear for two minutes until he saw sirens flashing in his rearview mirror. "Oh shit!"

"What happened?" Kat panicked.

"That dick is coming our way fast with the siren on!"

Sincere mashed the gas pedal, and the Lexus gained speed so fast that the flashing lights were too far behind him to catch up. He made a right then a quick left, almost hitting a parked car. Finally, he pulled into the back of someone's house and shut the car off.

"We'll be safe right here for a minute." Sincere was out of breath from the excitement.

******

"There he is!" Detective Colon said when she saw the Lexus about four blocks ahead of her.

Her police vehicle was doing maximum speed, but it was no match for the horsepower of the foreign car. She saw him speed up and turn right at a corner. She turned that same corner but still got no sighting of the Lexus. She made another right instead of the left that Sincere made and the Lexus was gone.

"Fuck! I lost him!" She banged her hands on the steering wheel.

She wasn't sure if Chasity was even in the car at first. After she saw them speeding away from the flashing lights, it confirmed that she was in the Lexus.

Detective Colon drove around several blocks twice, passing the house where the Lexus was hidden. "Fuck it, it'll pop up," she squinted and shook her head, "It looks like I'm not the only one trying to catch up with you."

THOT

******

Chasity woke up in the trunk disoriented and confused. There was gray duct tape on her mouth, and her hands were tied in front of her. Kat made the mistake of not tying Chasity's hands behind her back, so she was able to remove the duct tape. Chasity tried to remember the last thing that happened. *I was meeting with Sincere to get some weed, and that's the last thing I remember.*

"Let me the fuck out of here!" she yelled as she banged on the inside of the trunk. "Let me out! Please! If it's money that you want, I have plenty of it. Just don't kill me, please!" Chasity pleaded.

Kat and Sincere were on the inside listening to her pleas. When she said the part about the money, that's when Sincere got out of the car. "That's my cue." He opened the trunk.

Chasity couldn't see who was standing there at first, because her eyes couldn't focus from being in the dark trunk. She squinted, and then there was another shape standing next to the big one. When her eyes finally adjusted to the light, Kat and Sincere stood before her. Chasity launched a hard kick to Kat's stomach and tried to get out of the trunk and run. Sincere caught her and pushed her back into the trunk.

"Where do you think you're going?"

"Fucking bitch!" Kat said, trying to get a punch off, but Sincere stopped her from doing so. "I'm going to fuck you up! Watch!" Kat declared.

"Give me the rope and the duct tape!" Sincere demanded. "We don't have time for this!"

She gave it to him, and he tied her hands behind her back. He also tied her feet, then duct taped her mouth again and shut the trunk. "Let's get her over to that spot I told you about," Sincere ordered.

"Don't you think we should wait a while? That cop could still be out there waiting for us to come out," Kat's eyes were wide as she rotated her head 360 degrees looking for any sign of a cop car.

"Walk out on the street and see if they're out there."

Kat walked up and down the street. There was no sign of the black unmarked police vehicle in sight.

"It looks clear," she informed him.

They drove straight to the remote abandoned warehouse. A chair was positioned in the middle of the large empty space. The spaced had no electricity, just the illumination of the full moon's light shining through a large window.

Sincere opened his trunk. "If you kick me, I'm going to fuck you up! So don't try anything." Chasity shook her head in agreement.

He untied her hands and feet, then he escorted her to the empty chair and took the duct tape from her mouth with one quick snatch. "Ouch!" Chasity protested from the burning pain.

Sincere stood in front of her. "You know what this is about?" he asked her.

"Not really, but if I had to guess I'd say it's about the money." Chasity wasn't stupid. She knew exactly why she was tied up.

"You guessed it! It's all about the money. Where is it? We know you got it."

Kat stood beside him. "Yeah, bitch! You was braggin' about all the money Vinny was giving you. I know you didn't spend it all, because he was spending his money on you after he gave you the $350,000."

"You know what you are?" Chasity paused. "You are a bottom feeder! Scum on the bottom of a sanitation worker's boot!"

Kat punched her in the mouth, drawing blood. "Keep talking shit! I'll knock all those pearly white teeth out of your mouth, 'ho!"

Chasity spat the blood from her mouth at her. "Untie me! We'll see if you can do that shit when my hands are free! Untie me, bitch!"

The raw, negative energy coming from Chasity didn't elude Kat. She wasn't so sure she wanted to square off with her in a fair fight right now. Chasity was known to be aggressive in fights. She had a reputation for beating up girls that slept on her because of her beauty.

Sincere knew Kat didn't want any parts of Chasity. "Chill, Kat! Let me deal with her. You're making it worse. I got this."

Kat stormed off to sit in the car.

"Listen. We can do this the easy way or the hard way." He took out a pocket knife and opened it. "Now, where is the money?"

"Sincere, you don't have to do this." She looked in his eyes with passion. "Remember all the times we shared? I cared for you—it wasn't just about the weed." She saw him thinking about her words. "We were cool . . . don't let this monkey ass 'ho influence you to do this. She's a sneaky ass bum bitch. She's the real reason Torian is dead."

"What you mean?" Sincere was curious to hear this.

"Kat is the one that told Vinny that I had Torian at the condo. That's the reason Torian is dead. Because that bitch got Vinny's number from my phone, and she was trying to take my place with him. She knew about the money. I thought she was my best friend. You knew she was my dog, now look how she gettin' down. She'll do the same thing to you, Sincere. She don't give a fuck. She'll do you dirty."

Sincere thought hard about what she was saying. Some of what she was saying made sense. He knew Kat and Chasity were road dogs. They were inseparable at one time. When you saw one, the other was close.

"What happened between y'all that broke up the friendship?" Sincere asked.

"I'm telling you, Sincere, after I came up in the game with Vinny, she started secretly hating on me. I'm telling you the truth. She pretended to be my friend, but she was plotting my downfall." Chasity spoke quietly because she didn't want Kat to hear their conversation. "If you don't believe me, look in her phone. I bet she has all the messages she sent Vinny—snitching on me when she was supposed to be my homie. I bet this whole plan was her idea. I bet she told you I had $350,000, and that you can rob me for it."

Everything she was saying rang true and Sincere felt it. "You're right. She did tell me about the money. And she did influence me to rob you for the money." He was starting to have a change of heart.

"Look, untie me and ask her for her phone. Let's hold her down and go through her phone. If the messages aren't there, then you can tie me back up and do whatever. I'll give you the money anyway, but not that bitch. But you have to trust me, Sincere. She's the one that told Vinny that Torian was at the condo, and that's why he was murdered."

Sincere thought on her words and concluded that she was keeping it 100. Then he began to untie Chasity. "Okay, let's see if you're telling the truth."

They walked up to the passenger side door where Kat was listening to music. She didn't notice the two of them standing outside the door until Sincere tapped on the window. He opened the door.

"Let me see your phone," he demanded.

Her eyes widened at Chasity standing there untied. "What the fuck is going on?" Kat suddenly became offensive. "What the fuck you want to see my phone for? And why is this bitch untied? You were supposed to be finding out where the money is, not trying to get your dick sucked."

"Give me your phone, now!" Sincere snatched the Coach bag off her lap and went through it until he saw her phone. He started going through it.

"I don't know what she has him stored under, but I know his number. It's 631-995-9979," Chasity said.

Sincere dialed the number and a name popped up. It said 'Vin Trap.' He went into the messages to that number and lo and behold, there were text messages. The last message was on the day Torian was murdered. It read:

To: Vin Trap:

If u hurry u can catch her in the act. She's on her way 2 the condo with Torian as we speak.

That's all Sincere needed to see. "Get the fuck out of my car, 'ho!" He grabbed her by the arm and slung her to the ground. "You got my best friend murdered! You fucking sneaky ass bitch! Then you tried to turn me against Cherry by telling me how she got Torian killed when it was you."

"I don't know what you're talking about." The look of fear on her face was obvious. "I didn't do anything! She's lying!"

"Lying about what? Let's hear this." She didn't know she was caught red-handed. "See, I was just trying to look out for Torian. Know what I'm saying? She was manipulating him, can't you see that!"

"Now you're just freestyling," Chasity said. "I know everything, Kat. You were the one that told Vinny I would be at the condo with Torian the day he was murdered. So you're the one that got him killed! If you wouldn't have been a sneaky, conniving 'ho, Torian would still be here!"

Chasity rushed Kat and kicked her in the jaw. She mounted her and commenced to punching her in the face. "You fucking stupid bitch! You fucking killed my man! You killed my man!" With each word she hit Kat harder. "I loved him! And you killed him!"

Blood spewed from Kat's mouth and nose. Both eyes were blackened and shut. Chasity beat Kat in and out of consciousness. She beat her until her arms were tired of swinging; she was forced to stop. Kat lay on the floor unable to move.

"That's enough, Cherry!" Sincere grabbed her. "You proved your point. Let's go."

Sincere escorted Chasity to the Lexus. She sat down in the passenger seat and took a deep breath. Disheveled, tears streaming and uncontrollably trembling.

"It's okay. It's over," Sincere said, trying to calm her.

They both left the scene, leaving Kat lying on the floor bleeding. Conscious but still unsettled, she got up and walked toward the Lexus.

"Wait! You can't leave me here like this!" Kat yelled to no avail. "That's fucked up, you bitch ass nigga! You're going to get yours! Both of you!"

While they were in the car, Sincere took the time to apologize. "I really want to say sorry for doing this to you. She kept convincing me that you got my best friend murdered. Then she told me about the money and that we should take it from you because you got Torian killed. That's the only reason I went along with it. I hope you can forgive me, Cherry."

Chasity was just happy she wasn't tied up and facing torture. "Don't mention it. I know she manipulated you into doing this. She pretended to be my friend the whole time, so I know how convincing she can be."

Sincere drove her back to her BMW. "I'm really sorry about this, Cherry."

"It's okay. I know what's up." She walked to her car and noticed the keys were gone. "Where the fuck are my keys? That's strange. I know I left my keys in the ignition. My phone is still here. Maybe Kat has my keys?"

"I didn't see her take the keys. Do you have a spare key?" Sincere asked.

"Yes, but it's at the condo. Mind giving me a lift to the condo?"

"That's the least I can do."

She grabbed her phone and jumped back into the Lexus. *Oh yeah! It's on and fucking popping bitches! I got something for all you motherfuckers!* Chasity shook her head.

Sincere glanced at her as he drove. "Are you okay?"

"I'm good, it's ALL good."

******

Detective Colon was sitting at her desk when her phone beeped indicating that Chasity was moving again. "There she goes!" She jumped up to leave when she saw Detective Thomas. "Hey, Thomas, you want to go out for lunch?" She winked.

"Sure, why not."

They left the precinct but not headed for lunch. They had other plans in mind, plans that included Chasity.

CHAPTER 16

There's Only One Way Out!

"You good, or you want me to wait?" Sincere asked as they pulled up to the gate.

"I'm good. I'll just take a cab back to the park to get my car." She was feeling some type of way about what Sincere did to her.

"I hope you can really forgive me. You know I wouldn't have done some shit like that if it wasn't for Kat gassing me." He looked at her with mock sincerity.

"I'm good, but let me tell you something." She got out of the car. "As far as me giving you money, I wouldn't give you two dimes. Not even to rub together if it would save your life! You lucky I'm not in the mood to have you fucked up. So take that as your reward for letting me go. And next time you see me, just keep it moving."

With that being said, she walked up to the security guard at the post by the gate. The security guard was already standing outside when he noticed Chasity. The entire security staff knew a double homicide had taken place in her condo two days ago.

"Is everything okay, Miss Cherry?" Her disheveled appearance told him she'd been in a scuffle.

"Yeah, I'm good. But if you ever see that car lurking around here, call me."

"Will do, Miss Cherry." He lifted the gate. "Would you like to borrow the golf cart to take you to your condo?"

"That actually sounds like a good idea because I've been through a rough night."

Chasity drove the golf cart to the back of the complex where her unit was located. She always hid a spare key to the condo taped to the bottom of the screen door. When she opened the door she was immediately taken back to that day. A queasy feeling settled in the pit of her stomach as images of Torian lying dead with his eyes wide open ran through her mind. His blank stare tormented her. Then she saw Vinny slumped against the wall with his neck almost detached from his head.

She ran to the bathroom and stuck her head in the toilet and barfed so hard a vein popped out on her left temple. "I have to get the fuck out of this condo!"

Chasity stripped out of all of her clothes and turned on the shower. She got in and lathered up her washcloth, rubbing her body as hard as she could. She rubbed until her yellow skin turned red and cried as she scrubbed. The tears blended in with the water from the shower, both cleansing. *Was it all worth it? The cars and the money, the condo. Was it worth it? The way I've been living my life, selling my body for a couple hundred dollars! Is that all I'm worth? Can't cry about it now, this is what I wanted.*

She cried as she tried to wash away all of her discretions. Her ringing phone brought her back to reality. Quickly, she rinsed off the soap and grabbed a towel and dried off. By the time she reached the phone she'd missed the call. She wasn't able to see who it was because her screen was still cracked.

"I'm buying a new phone today. I'm changing my number, and I'm changing my life."

She threw on a gray Marc Jacobs sweat suit and some white and gray Chanel sneakers. Chasity stopped to look at herself in the mirror, and she didn't like what she saw. She wrapped her hair up in a bun and turned her head from side to side.

"That's better."

After using her house phone to call a cab, she looked around and the images began to flash again. "Fuck this!"

Grabbing her Louis Vuitton duffle bag, she opened her closet and began taking things out and stuffing them into the bag. When Chasity finished filling up the duffle bag, she grabbed the Gucci suitcase and filled that up. She had a few MCM backpacks, so she filled one up with shoes. Also, she retrieved a hidden stash of cash behind the headboard of her massive king-sized bed. There was only $10,000, but it was enough to replace whatever she was leaving behind. She put the MCM backpack on and held the Louis Vuitton in one hand and the Gucci in the other and carried them to the golf cart.

"Good-bye, condo! It was nice while it lasted, but Cherry got to go!" She slammed the door.

When she got to the gate, the cab was there waiting.

"Let me help you with that, Miss Cherry," the security guard offered.

"Thank you, Lawrence. You've been nothing but kind to me since I moved here." She reached in her bag and grabbed $300. "Here, take this."

"No, Miss Cherry, I can't," he protested.

She unbuttoned the chest pocket on his security uniform and stuffed the bills inside. "I insist."

"Thank you so much, Miss Cherry." He smiled.

"No, thank you." She jumped in the cab and said, "Take me to Timberline Park please."

A black unmarked Crown Victoria parked half a block up. Someone inside had been watching and waiting for her to come out.

*****

"So what you're telling me is that your brother-in-law had over $3 million in the bank, and he withdrew it all and gave it to a prostitute?" Detective Thomas couldn't wrap his thoughts around it.

"That's exactly what I'm telling you. Now my little cousin is left with two children and no money. She needs that money to take care of his children. It's only right that the money is left to his children and not some two-bit slut!" She got mad talking about it. "It's all cash, and she knows where it's at," Detective Colon assured him.

"Well, according to your GPS she's in that complex. When she comes out, let's just turn on the sirens and pull her over and arrest her. Once she's in cuffs, we can get her in the back of the cruiser and take her somewhere and get the info we need." He made it sound simple.

"There she goes!" Detective Colon snapped to attention and turned the car on.

"Let's wait until we get her driving. If we do it in front of witnesses, there's a chance we could go down. Let's be smart."

"You're right. I'm letting the fact that it's family cloud my judgment." She took a deep breath.

They watched Chasity and the security guard load the trunk of the cab. They saw her put the money in his chest pocket, and then she jumped in the cab.

"We don't have to be too close to her, because wherever she's going we'll know." Detective Thomas was a twenty-five year vet as opposed to Detective Colon's ten years on the force.

They waited for the cab to get some distance before they pulled off. She drove at a far distance from the cab at a slow cruise. The cab was moving fast to its destination.

"It looks like she's going toward Timberline Park," Detective Thomas said.

"That's where she left her car. I presume she's going back to get it. I have the keys." She dangled them. "I took them out yesterday. Luckily for her, because she left it running."

"You told me that Detective Samuels has been meeting up with her. That could mean a couple of things," Detective Thomas said. "One, he could be protecting her from people like us. Or two, he's just trying to get some sex. She is a good-looking woman."

Detective Colon frowned at his last statement. "We'll just have to keep an eye out for him."

The red dot stopped for two minutes, and then it started moving again. "She must've unloaded the luggage into her car. Now she's on the move again. We'll be looking for a midnight black BMW 645i," Detective Colon informed him while perspiring from anticipation.

I got you now bitch!

******

"I don't have a tip for you today. Sorry," Chasity said as the cab came to a stop. She gave him exact change.

Chasity got out of the cab and popped the trunk of the BMW. The trunk of the cab was already open. The cab driver was on the phone, and he made no attempt to help her. After she put the luggage in the trunk of the BMW, Chasity got into her car and pressed the pedal to the metal. She drove straight to Smith Haven Mall to buy a new phone. She got out and ran inside.

When she got to the Apple store, there was a long line so she had to wait. "It's always crowded in here!" she protested to the dismay of the patrons in line.

She looked at her Rolex. It was 6:30 p.m. She looked around to see if she was being followed. Everyone was suspect because she didn't know who else was working with Detective Colon. She bit her nails as she waited.

"Excuse me, miss."

Chasity jumped as she turned to see who was tapping her shoulder.

"Sorry if I startled you." the Apple store worker offered, noticing Chasity's demeanor.

"It's okay." Chasity took a deep breath and closed her eyes for a moment.

"There's a shorter line opening up right over there."

"Thank you."

I have to relax or I'm going to go crazy!

******

Detective Colon drove around the parking lot of Smith Haven Mall. "Damn! It was your bright idea to stay far behind her!" she said to Detective Thomas.

"Do you want to do this the smart way? Or the sloppy way? All we need is some civilian seeing us apprehend her, and that's her witness, unless we kill her after we get the money." He looked at her for a reaction and was surprised when she didn't dispute killing her. *She's obsessed with this chick.*

"There it is!" Detective Colon spotted the BMW. "Let's just park behind her and wait for her to come out. This time I'm staying within eyesight of her." She glanced at her watch. It was 6:33 p.m. Briefly, Detective Colon thought about why she was doing all this in the first place. *The money! Yeah, I'm doing it for my cousin too, so she can take care of the kids. But I got to get mine off the top!*

She knew her cousin would hit her off with a nice piece for helping her. Detective Colon just wanted to get ahead for once. A cop's salary is under $100,000 per year. She wanted to buy expensive things without worrying about her finances.

After we get this money, I'm going on vacation. "What the fuck is this bitch doing?" Detective Colon grew aggravated after forty-five minutes had passed.

Detective Thomas was becoming annoyed about her attitude. *Why did I agree to help this crazy bitch*? he thought.

"Wait a minute! The red dot on my GPS disappeared! What the fuck is going on?" Detective Colon was instantly in panic mode.

"Relax, she's probably in a bad area and has no reception."

"Let's hope that's what it is."

"There she goes!" Detective Colon started her car. "Contrary to your theory, the red dot didn't show up. And she's right in front of us." At exactly 6:47 p.m. Chasity was running to her car.

This time Detective Colon stayed two cars behind her.

"I'm not letting you out of my sight this time." She was used to Chasity driving at a fast speed. Chasity made a right toward the entrance to the Long Island Expressway, and when she got into the third lane the car leaped into turbo.

"She's getting away!" Detective Thomas said when he saw how fast her car took off.

"Not this time!" Detective Colon threw on the siren and mashed the gas pedal, seeing how far ahead Chasity was, but the Crown Victoria was gaining on the BMW.

******

Chasity looked in her rearview mirror and saw flashing lights coming her way fast. "Fuck! The last thing I need is a speeding ticket!" She didn't slow down at first. "Maybe they're after someone else."

The Crown Victoria sped up and was three cars behind her, blowing the horn for cars to move out of the way. Once the cars moved, the cruiser accelerated until it was right on her bumper.

"Fuck! They were coming for me!" She slowed down and pulled over.

Chasity knew the drill, so she started taking her driver's license and registration out. She looked in her rearview and almost choked when she saw Detective Colon. "You! What the fuck is going on?"

She thought about what Detective Samuels told her. *Why would she put her job in jeopardy to interrogate you? She's a narcotics detective, not a homicide detective. She's out of her jurisdiction.*

"Just stay cool," she said to herself, right before Detective Colon reached the driver's side door. "What's the problem, officer?"

"The problem is that you were doing 120 miles an hour. Who're you trying to get away from?" She motioned with her fist as if to strike Chasity but held it back. Then she tried to open the door but it was locked.

"Why the fuck are you trying to open my door? Am I under arrest? If not, just give me a speeding ticket and let me be on my way."

Detective Colon pulled out her service weapon. "Get the fuck out of the car!"

"For what? I didn't do anything." Chasity was shaken with the fear of being shot.

"Get the fuck out of the car now!" Detective Colon demanded.

"You're not going to tell me why? After you attacked me at the precinct, now you're playing a traffic cop. Before, you were playing a homicide detective when we were in the precinct."

She tried to open the door again. "I'm warning you! If you don't get out of the car I'm going to shoot you!"

Chasity looked her in her eyes. "No you're not!" She put the car in drive and pressed the gas to the floor. Detective Colon tried to grab the door handle just as she accelerated. The BMW took off so fast Detective Colon sprang her thumb trying to hold on to it.

"Fuck! My fucking thumb!" Detective Colon held the throbbing digit.

Chasity thought about calling Detective Samuels, but her new phone wiped away all of her contacts.

"Damn!" she shouted. "Just when I need him!"

She dipped through traffic like a NASCAR professional. She looked in her rearview, and they were a half mile behind.

"I need to call Tommy." She requested Siri's assistance on her iPhone. "Siri, get me the number to Homicide Detective Samuels from the third precinct."

"One moment," Siri responded.

In thirty seconds flat the phone was ringing. "Detective Samuels speaking."

"Tommy! It's me. Cherry. I need your help—"

*****

Detective Samuels abruptly hung up. He looked at the caller ID and wrote the number down. He grabbed his coat and dashed to his cruiser.

Once he was in his cruiser, he dialed the number from his cell phone. "Hello? Cherry?"

"I'm in a high speed chase! Detective Colon tried to pull me over and arrest me. She put a gun in my face and ordered me to get out of my car or she'd shoot me! I put the car in drive and burned rubber. She's a half mile behind me! What the fuck do I do?"

"Try to relax. If you can get away from the highway and get to a populated area, you'll be safe. She knows she can't touch you around other civilians because they're witnesses."

"Okay, I'm getting off on Deer Park Ave headed toward the Tanger Outlets."

"I'll meet you there in fifteen minutes," Detective Samuels said before hanging up.

******

"She's getting off on Deer Park Ave!" Detective Colon shouted.

"You have to remember, this is off the books, so we can't just do this in front of witnesses. I'm not jeopardizing my career for this shit!" Detective Thomas wanted out, but it was too late.

She paid him no mind. The only thoughts that mattered to her at the moment was catching Chasity. What he said was irrelevant.

"There she is!" They were four cars behind Chasity. "Looks like she's headed toward the outlets. She thinks she'll be safe there."

"What the fuck do you mean 'she thinks she'll be safe there!' She will be safe there! I'm out! I'm not doing this with you! You can let me out of the fucking car right here!" Detective Thomas was fuming.

Detective Colon all but ignored him and kept driving. "It's over when *I* say it's over!" she replied.

"Are you out of your fucking mind? Stop the fucking car!"

She kept driving, but there was a stoplight up ahead. Chasity made the light but Detective Colon didn't. She turned on the siren and went right through the light, almost causing a major collision.

"You are fucking insane! You almost caused an accident! Pull over right now!" Detective Thomas demanded. "I'm not playing anymore!" He pulled out his weapon and pointed it at her.

"So what, you're going to shoot me now?" she asked him calmly.

"No! I'm demanding that you pull over and let me out of this car!"

She kept driving and followed Chasity to the parking lot of the Tanger Outlets. Chasity quickly parked and ran into the crowded outdoor outlet mall. She got lost for a second, but Detective Colon spotted her from behind.

Their eyes met once Chasity looked back to see where she was. The detective gave chase as Chasity took off running at full speed through the busy shoppers, out of Detective Colon's view.

"Shit! She's getting away!" Detective Colon ran, hoping to catch up to her, but she was nowhere in sight. "Where the fuck is she?"

******

Chasity ran to the bathroom and hid in a stall. She took out her cell phone and called the last number in her call log: Detective Samuels. He picked up on the first ring.

"This crazy bitch is trying to hunt me down! Please get here fast!" Chasity spoke in a low tone just in case Colon had entered the bathroom.

"Calm down. Where are you now?" he asked.

"I'm in the bathroom stall on the side by the Ralph Lauren store."

"I just pulled in. I'm headed toward the Ralph Lauren store right now. What I need you to do is come out and casually walk into the store and wait for me. I'll be right behind you."

She took a deep breath and exited the stall. When she came out onto the walkway she looked both ways. Chasity was almost face to face with Detective Colon.

"Oh shit!" She trotted to the Ralph Lauren store.

As soon as she entered, she was greeted. "Hello. Can I help you with anything?"

"Yes, as a matter of fact you can." Chasity looked back through the window. Detective Colon was headed straight toward the Ralph Lauren store.

Just before Detective Colon stood within ten yards of the entrance, Detective Samuels entered the store. He didn't see Detective Colon because of the angle in which he entered. But she saw him.

"What the fuck is he doing here?" Detective Colon stopped in her tracks. "Captain Save-a-ho to the rescue again!" Her nose flared and her face turned crimson from anger.

******

Chasity's eyes lit up when she saw Detective Samuels. She flung her arms open and hugged him. "Thank you so much for coming. I'm telling you, she pulled me over and put her gun in my face and ordered me to get out. She said I'm under arrest, but when I asked her for what she didn't say anything. That's when I knew she was going to kill me." Chasity was visibly shaken by the ordeal.

"I'm here now." He rubbed her hair as he spoke. "No one can harm you now."

As he hugged her, she looked over his shoulder through the window. Detective Colon stood there watching them embrace. Seething with anger, she shook her head and stormed away.

"Let's get out of here," Detective Samuels said. "Let's take my car just in case. I can bring you back to your car later."

"Good idea," Chasity said, grateful he'd shown up when he had.

******

When Detective Colon got back to the cruiser, Detective Thomas was gone. He'd caught a cab back to the precinct.

"Fucking coward!"

She waited an hour for Chasity to get back in her BMW, but after another thirty minutes, she knew she wasn't coming back to her car anytime soon. She drove back to the precinct. As soon as she sat at her desk, Detective Thomas rushed past her office trying to avoid her, but she made that impossible.

"Can we talk?" Detective Colon wanted to smooth things over. "I know I was a little erratic, but you understand? Right?" She smiled to get the best reaction, but it didn't work.

"You're a sick, twisted, crazy bitch. I want no parts of your twisted plans. Let's forget we even spoke on it." He walked away.

You think you're out. There's only one way for you to be out. You know too much, buddy. I'm not taking the risk of you talking. She sat at her desk with a pen in her hand and wrote on a piece of paper: *Take care of Detective Thomas.*

CHAPTER 17

What's Done in the Dark!

What the fuck am I going to do if I don't get that money! Jenny Vitaly didn't like to speak out loud about her money problems around the kids. But she was down to her last thousand dollars. *Something has to give!*

Jenny stood by the bus stop with her two sons waiting for their school bus to arrive. It was their morning ritual Monday thru Friday and again in the afternoon when they got off the bus. She looked at Vinny Jr. *God, he resembles his father so much.*

"I really want that new Xbox One!" Anthony said in a whining tone. "You said we'll be able to get things real soon. When is real soon going to get here?" The youngest, Anthony, looked more like her and inherited her temperament.

"Anthony, you're going to have to wait, sweetheart. Times are a little rough right now, so you'll just have to bear with me, honey." A lump formed in Jenny's throat.

It was breaking her heart to hear her ten-year-old son speak like this. When Vinny was alive they wanted for nothing. Even if he spent most of his time with Chasity, he made sure they had everything they ever wanted. Jenny was content with the arrangement. She'd long ago stopped being attracted to Vinny. However, she loved him because of the kids. Other than that, she couldn't care less who he was screwing around with. Jenny was no fool; she had some secrets of her own.

The bus pulled up and opened its door. There were ten kids and parents standing around waiting. The kids boarded the bus single file. Vinny Jr. was the last child to get on the bus. Before he got on he looked back at his mother.

"I love you, Mom," Vinny said. He stepped onto the bus.

"I love you too, VJ." Jenny blew him a kiss. The bus doors shut and after thirty seconds it took off.

She walked back to her mini-mansion and got ready for her weekly rendezvous. After showering she put on a leopard print one-piece nightgown. Jenny wore nothing under it but her soft olive-colored skin. Jenny was not an ugly woman. On the contrary she was good looking. Why Vinny was no longer attracted to her was a question her secret lover asked often. He thought Jenny's 38DD breasts were perfect. Her ass was small, but it was exactly how her lover liked it. She had a pretty face with emerald eyes that shined when she smiled. Her hair was dyed bleach blonde, which made her resemble Pamela Anderson. Although she had two children, her stomach was as flat as an ironing board.

Jenny looked at the clock. "He should be here any minute." Her secret lover was always on time for their weekly appointments.

She sprayed perfume on and looked at her reflection. "Not bad for a thirty-eight-year-old mother of two."

Ding-dong!

"That's him!" She rushed to the door and opened it. "Hey baby! I missed you." She hugged Rocco tight and kissed him with her tongue.

Rocco received her and responded by putting his tongue deep into her mouth. "I missed you too! I've been so busy at this new construction site. All I can think about is fucking you!"

He entered the house and lifted Jenny in his arms and carried her to the bedroom. He tossed her on the bed and started taking his clothes off. His penis was already hard, so Jenny took the opportunity to take him in her mouth and suck until she felt him about to erupt.

"Not yet." She stopped the flow of semen from exploding into her mouth. "I need you in my pussy!" She stood up and pushed him on the bed. Then she mounted him, riding him like a cowgirl.

"Yes!" Rocco screamed out. "I missed this fucking pussy! Ride that cock!"

"Oh my god! It feels so good! I want it all the time, baby!"

"Yes! Me too!" Rocco responded. "I'm about to cum!"

"Wait! Let's cum together!" She sped up her movement. "You ready, baby?"

"Yes!"

She rode him harder and faster, feeling the buildup in his thrust. She kept in tune with his movement, until a warm stream of semen entered her vagina. And he felt the warmth of her cum wash over his penis.

"That's so good!" he confessed. "I can't get enough."

"I'm cumming!" Her body contorted and her eyes closed. "Oh fuck, I'm cumming."

Her body fell to the side, and she lay there enjoying the effects of the morning sex session. Rocco did the same, and lay panting from the after effects of a great sexual escapade. Both were enamored by the other's sexual ability. The attraction was strong, and the vibe was there. The only thing askew was Rocco's close relation to Vinny. They were first cousins.

Rocco and Jenny had been secretly in an affair for the past six months. It all began when Vinny started spending more time with Chasity. Rocco knew that Vinny was cheating on Jenny, and he thought of Jenny as a sexy woman that any man would want. He didn't understand why Vinny wasn't attracted to her. Because he surely found everything about Jenny fascinating and sexy.

She lay there thinking about the first time they hooked up. "I'm so glad that you came over that day and rescued me," Jenny said. "I remember it like it was yesterday. I was just getting out of the shower when you rang the doorbell."

"That's the day I couldn't take it anymore. I was trying to tell Vinny to stop seeing this girl and giving her all his money. He told me if I didn't like it I didn't have to deal with him. I pushed him and got in my truck and drove straight to your house."

Rocco rang the doorbell. Jenny, wearing only a robe, stood at the door in seconds. "Hey Rocco, what's up? Is everything okay?" His heavy breathing and angry snarl communicated his attitude. "Come in."

". . . Vinny, he's an asshole!" He was so mad he couldn't get it out. "I mean, you're so beautiful. Why does he have to cheat on you?" He looked into her green eyes and moved toward her and kissed her.

"This isn't right, Rocco," Jenny said, but she didn't stop kissing him. "Stop, please." But she was the one who continued kissing him.

"I think you're one of the most beautiful women on earth!" He held her face in his hands as he kissed her. "I want you so bad. I've always wanted you. Vinny doesn't deserve you."

"You're right!" Jenny kissed him back harder. "I've always wanted you too, Rocco." She untied her robe and let it fall to the floor. Rocco took her right there in her living room for the first time. And he showed up to her house three times a week to repeat it ever since.

"That's the best thing I ever did in my life. I know it was wrong, but it felt so damn right. Now that Vinny is gone"—he looked into her eyes—"I was thinking that we can make it official. I'm tired of hiding how I feel about you. I want to go to sleep and wake up to you every day for the rest of my life. I want to marry you." Rocco knew he was reaching, but he had to tell her how he really felt.

"I feel the same way, Rocco, but I'm not ready to tell the boys and the family that I'm in love with my deceased husband's first cousin." She shook her head. "No, this isn't right. We can't tell the family about this. We'll be lepers, regardless of how people act in our presence; they'll always talk trash behind our backs. I'm not ready for that."

"We can leave and no one will know." He sounded desperate. "I don't care what they think!" Rocco stood and began pacing around the living room. He was a very muscular man, so his presence was already menacing. "If anyone has anything to say about it, I'll handle it!" He swung a punch into the wall and left a huge crater.

"Rocco! Calm down, baby." Jenny's eyes shifted from side to side in confusion. Her heart began to race; she'd never seen Rocco act like this. "I'm just saying that I'm not ready to let the family know yet." She stood and hugged him. "I'm here. I'm not going anywhere. Just give me some time."

Rocco took deep breaths to calm himself. "You're right, Jen. I'll wait, but not for long. In six months I want you and the kids to move into my house. And I'll take care of you."

"Speaking of taking care of things, do you think you can give me some money? Anthony keeps bugging me about a new Xbox One. The freaking thing costs $600, and I'm down to my last."

"Not a problem." He reached into his pocket and pulled out a wad of hundred dollar bills. "Here's $2,000. Don't spend it all in one place." He put the remaining cash back in his pocket. "By the way, what's the deal with the broad that has his cash? I know you told me your cousin was handling it, but if you want me to get a couple of my goons on it, just say the word."

"Hmm, you know what. I'll take you up on that offer. My cousin keeps blundering the job at every turn. Maybe you will make better progress." She kissed him. "Matter of fact, I know you'll have better results. Go get my money for me, baby. And I promise we can live happily ever after as a family like you want."

"Say no more, Jenny." Rocco's mood transformed in an instant. "Consider it done." He put his clothes on and headed for the door, stopping to get a kiss. "You know I love you, right?"

"Of course, baby." She closed her eyes and kissed him. "And I love you too."

Jenny's cell phone rang. She picked it up from the counter. "Hold on, let me answer this call." She pressed 'ANSWER' upon seeing her cousin's name on the display. "What's up?"

"You forgot we were supposed to go down to the funeral home today to prepare for Vinny's funeral?"

"Oh shit!"

"Oh shit is right. Because I just pulled up, and I see Rocco's truck in the driveway."

"He was just here to drop off some of Vinny's personal stuff from the office."

"Yeah, okay. Well, I'm giving you fifteen minutes to get ready." Detective Colon hung up.

Jenny peeped through the window shade to see if she was really at her house. When she saw her signature unmarked cruiser, she gasped and hung the phone up. "Fuck!"

"What just happened?" Rocco asked curiously.

"My cousin Jenny just pulled up and saw your truck in the driveway. She's a fucking detective. She's going to know something is going on between us. I know her." Jenny was nervous about anyone finding out their secret.

"So, let her find out. Soon we'll be living together and everyone will know. If they don't like it, they don't have to come around."

"Yeah, you're right." Jenny said that to appease Rocco. "You better get going." She kissed him one last time.

"See you next week?" he asked.

"Yep, next week."

Rocco strolled to his truck and waved at Detective Colon. She nodded in acknowledgment, but noticed his peculiar movements; they had the smell that told Detective Colon that something was fishy.

"Let me find out little Jenny is fucking her husband's cousin." She took a sip of the 7-Eleven coffee. "That would be some fucked up, messy shit."

******

While Jenny dressed, she reflected on Rocco's words and the way he acted. It scared her because he went from 0 to 100 real quick. She'd never witnessed Rocco become violent, but one thing was for sure, she didn't like it.

I don't think I can deal with a man that has a temper like that. He could snap my neck if he ever lost control the way he did today. After he helps me get my money, I'll have to let him down nice and easy somehow. Because what he displayed today was a total turn off.

I can't put my finger on it, but something just wasn't right about the way Rocco flipped out. I'm not trying to find out what it is by having my skull caved in. I'll pass on that one, buddy. Besides, I don't want to come out of the shadows about us to my sons, and then the family. I know how they are, traditional Italian values. That shit would disrupt the order, and I'm not about to be the one to do it.

She finished getting dressed and ran out to Detective Colon's car and got in. Detective Colon gave Jenny a suspicious look. "I really hope you're not messing around with Rocco. You know how disgusting that will look."

"I'm not, *okay!*" she snapped, giving way to more suspicion. "I told you he came by to drop off some of Vinny's things. Now, can we get this over with? It's not like we're going to the mall." Jenny counted to five before she began to cry to throw Detective Colon off the trail.

"It's okay, little cuz. Big Cuz is here for you." She reached across the seat to rub her shoulder. "I'm sorry if I upset you. Let's get down to the funeral home. They're waiting on us."

Jenny rolled her eyes but her big cuz missed the gesture. Any quirk or misstep from a lover or friend easily annoyed Jenny, a character trait of her scorpion birth sign. Once she's turned off, it's a wrap. That's why it was so easy for her to allow Vinny to do his thing. Long ago she'd been turned off by him. Rocco wasn't the only fling she'd had; her former lover turned her off too, and she'd cut him off with the quickness. The same way she was about to do with Rocco—cut him off at the head.

******

Rocco drove himself straight to the gym to let off some steam. He wasn't feeling the fact that Jenny wasn't ready to come out about their relationship. He was used to getting his way with women because he was muscular and had lots of money. When Jenny expressed her hesitation about living with him, it sent him over the edge, and he knew why. It didn't solely have to do with Jenny's response.

He entered the Power House gym and went straight to the locker room. In his locker was a syringe and three different types of anabolic steroids. He put the syringe into the bottle and extracted the substance. Then he went into the bathroom stall and injected himself in his buttocks and waited a few minutes. (ACTION!) He exited the stall and returned the syringe to the locker.

Ever since his mid-twenties, Rocco had been using steroids. Now at the age of thirty-five he was a mass of artificial muscle. Jenny heard stories about Rocco going off, but she didn't relate it to steroids. To Italians, acting extra tough was part of the culture, so it was natural. He, however, knew it affected his mood and his anger was getting worse. He also knew why he'd punched the wall at Jenny's house. Rocco had increased the quantity to harmful levels. He was going through something mentally and emotionally, so he felt he had to up his dosage to workout harder, to compete with the younger guys. It boosted his ego and his self-esteem.

With steroids in his system, he was in beast mode and would lift all the weights in the gym. He started off with the bench press. After a light warm-up set, he put four plates on each side totaling 405 pounds. He slowly got on the bench and put his hands on the bar, ready to lift the massive amount of weight. The younger muscle heads were watching. It was always a competition amongst bodybuilders in the gym. Rocco knew he had to show off because they were observing him.

"Huh!" he let out a loud sound of brute strength as he lifted 405 pounds out the gate and on its way down to touch his chest, then back up. He did the first one slow. A burst of human energy and strength took over, and he lifted 405 pounds for fifteen reps, before putting it back in the gate.

"He's a beast!" one of the younger bodybuilders said. "That's the most reps I've ever seen anyone do with 405 pounds."

Rocco worked out for two hours until the steroids teetered off in his system. He took a shower and left the building. When he got to his truck, he went through his phone contacts until he found a name that read 'Fox.' He pressed the call button.

"Hey, Rocco! I always know the nature of your calls," Fox stated. "You want to meet me down at Shananigans Bar & Grill in an hour so we can talk?"

"Sure, I'll see you there in an hour." Rocco hung up. "Take care of this fucking slut once and for all!"

He drove off from the gym to meet Shawn Fox. They nicknamed him the Fox because he didn't make a sound when he crept up on his victims and snuffed out their life. This time it was a little different; he needed someone apprehended. Whatever the job was, Fox was the best.

Rocco pulled into the parking lot of Shananigan's and gazed around before getting out. Using steroids often made Rocco paranoid. He locked his truck and entered the bar and looked for Fox. He saw him playing a game of pool with some nondescript guy. Rocco took the time to order a drink to take the edge off.

"Come on, old man! You can play better than that. I don't want to take advantage of my elders," the younger man said, taunting Fox.

"Old man!" Fox hated to be called an old man. "I'll show you an old man, young punk!" Fox put the seven ball in the right corner pocket.

"Oh shit! Grandpa trying to come back!"

Fox shot two more back to back. "Looks like Grandpa is about to take the whole game. Eight ball in the left side pocket." He shot it in smooth. "Game! Give me my $100."

The young man pulled a crisp $100 bill out of his wallet. "You got that one. Let's play another game. Double or nothing?"

"I have some business to attend to, kid. Maybe next time." Fox strolled off, leaving the young man with a bruised ego.

"What's going on, Fox? It's been a while since we spoke," Rocco said with a firm handshake.

"Sometimes I think it's better that way. Considering."

Rocco showed Fox a picture in his phone. "Her name is Cherry. I need her apprehended and put up somewhere safe until I get there."

"Do you need me to dispose of her afterward?"

"Most likely, because I might have to torture her for information," Rocco answered with a twitch in his eye.

"Where can I find her?"

"Here is a list of places she frequents. You can catch her at any one of these places on any given moment." Rocco kept a list in his phone. "I'll text you the pic and the info."

"That'll help." Fox admired the picture of Cherry. "When is the deadline?"

"Two weeks tops." Rocco gulped down his drink.

"I'm on it."

Rocco got up to leave and gave him a serious look. "This is very important to me. Don't fuck this up." .

"When have I ever let you down, Rock?"

"Never." Rocco walked out of the bar and got back in his truck and pulled off.

He thought about being with Jenny after he pulled off the task of helping her get Vinny's money. He had become obsessed with Jenny in a bad way. Rocco was a ticking time bomb, and Jenny's refusal would be the trigger to ignite him.

"It won't be long until we're together. Nothing is going to get in the way."

CHAPTER 18

I Can Get Used to This!

Detective Samuels sat at his desk scrolling down the computer screen reading the information he'd requested from Google. He'd spent the past three days investigating Vincent Vitaly and the Vitaly Construction Empire. What he discovered put the pieces of this puzzle together in an uncanny way. *I can make sense out of most of this mystery. Chasity has to fill in the blanks,* he thought.

"I need to get in contact with Cherry immediately." He dialed her number, and she answered on the first ring. "Cherry, we have to talk—in person."

"What is it?" Chasity had been through so much in the past three days. She was about to panic at the sound of more drama. "Please don't tell me something fucked up right now; my nerves can't take it."

"It's nothing for you to worry about. I just need to talk to you face to face about some new discoveries you might find interesting."

"Come to the Radison on Motor Parkway. Room 515."

"I'll be there in twenty minutes." He hung up and rushed to his car.

******

Chasity sat on the edge of the bed in her hotel suite all alone. She'd been having the same dream lately. She couldn't make sense of it. It was the same dream where Torian stood by a lone huge oak tree in a field of red roses. When she tried to get close, he'd hide behind the tree disappearing from her sight. She didn't want to fall asleep for fear of having the dream. *What are you trying to tell me, Torian?*

To calm her worry, she rolled up a fat blunt and walked out to the balcony and lit it up. Slowly, she took pulls of the blunt while in deep thought. *I've made some profound changes in my life since the incident with Vinny and Torian. For one, I haven't had sex since that day. Second, I'm totally free from selling sex over the Internet. And I feel good about it!*

I never thought the day would come when I'd say I'm happy as hell that I'm not posting up on Front Page anymore. I remember that was my whole life. I didn't see anything wrong with it. Wow! How stupid was I? You couldn't pay me to get back into that life. I guess everything happens for a reason.

She finished the blunt just as someone was knocking on the door. She knew who it was because only one person knew her room number, Detective Samuels. She gave herself a once over in the mirror before opening the door.

"How are you doing, Cherry?" Fox said in a polite tone.

"Who the fuck are you?" Chasity yelled in surprise. "And how do you know my name?" She looked down and saw the 9-millimeter with a silencer attached to the barrel concealed under his trench coat.

He pushed the door open and stepped into the room and closed the door. "Get dressed. We're going for a little ride."

Chasity quickly put on her sneakers. She already had on sweat pants and a sweat shirt. She knew Detective Samuels would be there any minute, so she had to stall for time.

"Before you take me on my little ride, please let me use the bathroom. After all, you did scare the shit out of me." She moved toward the bathroom.

"Okay, but I want the door open, and I'm going to stand right outside watching you. So don't try anything funny. Got me?" Fox kept his weapon pointed toward her as he spoke.

"I got you. Just don't shoot me." She slowly pulled her pants down to her ankles. Fox smirked, enjoying the strip tease while she poked her round ass out to sit on the toilet. Realizing his attention was lacking, she stood and showed him her shaven vagina.

"You like that?" She smacked her vagina. "You know, you don't have to do this. You can have it all, the money, *and* the pussy." She smacked her vagina again.

"Hmm, that sounds like my kind of idea." He moved an inch.

Knock, knock, knock!

Fox turned his head toward the door, but he kept his gun extended toward, Chasity. Thinking quickly, she slammed the door on his arm, causing the gun to fall out of his hand onto the floor. While Fox was recovering from the hard blow to his elbow, Chasity grabbed the gun before Fox could.

With her pants still bunched around her ankles, she stood there pointing the gun at Fox. "Get your motherfucking ass over to that chair and sit down before I unload this whole clip into your fucking head!"

Knock! Knock! Knock!

"Cherry! Are you okay!" Detective Samuels said after hearing her voice boom from outside the door.

"Not really!" she responded.

Fox was holding his arm and moving slowly to the chair. Chasity moved at the same time, but toward the door. She opened it and Detective Samuels entered with his service weapon drawn.

"Who is this guy?" Detective Samuels asked in a surprised tone, seeing Fox sitting on a sofa chair holding his right arm.

"Good question. He knocked on the door, and I opened it thinking it was you, but he had this"—She held up the 9-millimeter with the silencer—"pointed at me."

"How did you unarm him?" Detective Samuels asked, intrigued.

"I told him I had to use the bathroom, and he was so caught up in staring at my pussy that I was able to slam the door on his arm. He dropped the gun and I picked it up."

Detective Samuels was impressed. "Good thing I came when I did." He got so close to Fox's face he could smell the onions on his breath. "Who sent you?"

"I don't know what you're talking about." Fox didn't flinch.

Pow!

Detective Samuels punched Fox in his mouth, knocking his front tooth loose. "I'm going to ask one more time. Who sent you?"

"You can punch me, stab me, hell, even shoot me, and I'll go to my grave with the answer. So do what you got to do." Fox showed no signs of fear.

Detective Samuels knew he couldn't arrest him because this was an informal visit. He could lose his job if they found out what he was doing. He had an idea.

"Stand up." Detective Samuels took out his cuffs and put them on Fox behind his back.

"I knew you was a fuckin' pig!" Fox protested. "I smelled you when you got in my face."

Detective Samuels punched Fox in his stomach and he bent over. "Watch your mouth." He escorted Fox to the bathroom and shut the door. Samuels then stood next to Chasity so he could speak in a low tone. "I came to tell you what I found out about The Vitaly Construction

Empire and Detective Colon and her involvement in this whole mess."

Chasity took a deep breath. "Lay it on me. I'm ready."

"Well, it appears that Detective Jenny Colon is the first cousin of Jenny Vitaly, the widow of the late Vincent Vitaly."

"So that's why she had the grudge against me. It all makes sense now." Chasity was actually relieved.

"That's not all. It seems the Vitaly Construction Empire is in deep water with the Federal Government for fraud, embezzlement, and tax evasion. They are the clean business branch of the Mafia. The Vitaly family is one of the most influential Italian families in America. The great grandfather, Vito Vitaly was a member of the original Commission in the 1930s. He escaped prosecution and started a construction business; the rest is history." He paused. "Which leads me to my next series of questions."

"What now?" Chasity became defensive.

"Is there something you haven't told me? Anything?" He was fishing.

"Yes, there's something I didn't tell you."

Caught something! he thought. "You have to be 100% honest and truthful from now on, or I'm not helping you anymore."

"Okay." She took another deep breath. "Vinny was taking all of his money out of the bank and storing it in a storage unit. And I'm the only one that knows where the money is, and I'm the only person with access to it."

"How much money are we talking about?"

"Close to $1.7 million in cash."

"That's the missing piece!" Detective Samuels abruptly stood up with a smile and a twinkle in his eyes. "I was trying to figure out a motive for Detective Colon to put her career on the line. It couldn't just be because the deceased was her cousin's husband. That wasn't a strong enough motive to me, but $1.7 million—now that's a motive."

"I figured out something as well." Chasity rubbed her head before speaking. "Vinny kept saying he wanted to take all his money out of the bank and go to another country. He had me believe that he wanted to leave the country to start over with me because his family didn't approve of us. Really it was because he knew they were under investigation, and he was going to skip town with the money before the Feds came to take it."

"That makes sense."

"Now everyone wants to get their hands on the money. Well, I'm not parting with one red cent!" Chasity declared. "I worked hard to get that money!"

"I don't think you understand what you're up against." He paused to say the right words. "The Vitaly Family are coldblooded murderers. They beat three murder cases in the '80s. That's how they were able to rise to the top of the construction business. They literally took out the competition. They will have no problem taking you out for that money."

Chasity realized the severity of the situation. "I'm scared, Tommy." She buried her face in his chest and cried. "I don't want to die over no money! They can have it! I just want to be left alone to live a normal life."

Detective Samuels hesitated, but he put his arms around her and held her. "It'll be okay. I won't let anything happen to you."

His words comforted her. She never had a real father figure in her life, so for her, any man who wanted to protect her became that figure. Right now it was Detective Samuels. He held her and she cried like a little girl.

"It's okay, Cherry. I'm here for you. I won't let you down."

She cried until she couldn't shed any more tears. She sighed in relief. "Thank you for being there for me."

"Don't mention it."

"No, really. No man has ever done anything for me if he wasn't getting something in return. Vinny did lots of things for me, but I had to have sex with him whenever he wanted it. I'm tired of living like that. That's why I'd rather do this alone if its sex you want."

"I can control myself, Cherry. The main thing is that you're all right." Detective Samuels held in his feelings for her. "I'm not going to lie and say that I'm not attracted to you, but I will respect your wishes and keep it strictly in the friend zone."

"I appreciate that, Tommy." She hoped sincerity rather than bullshit filled his declaration.

******

Fox was an escape artist. He kept handcuff keys stashed in his clothes just for moments like this. He kept one in his back pocket and one in his front. He reached for the key in his back pocket. He'd practiced escaping like this a thousand times, so it was a cinch. In two minutes flat he was out of the cuffs. Now he had to find a way out. Luckily for him there was a window in the bathroom that led to a four-foot landing.

"Perfect," he whispered.

Fox climbed through the window and jumped onto the landing. From there he was able to enter the building through a fire escape door and walked down the stairs to the lobby and exited the hotel.

"That was a close call." He held up his hand for a cab. "I have to be more careful."

He hopped in the first cab that stopped for him.

"Take me to Coventry Village in Central Islip, please."

"Got you." The cab driver drove off.

I might have lost her for now, but not for long. He thumbed his nose. "The Fox always gets his prey."

"You say something, boss?" The cab driver glanced at the rearview mirror to look at Fox.

"I was just thinking out loud."

******

Detective Samuels didn't want to leave without resolving what to do about Fox. He didn't want to kill him or assault him any more than he already had. He did want another crack at making him talk.

"I'd bet the whole $1.7 million that the guy in the bathroom was sent by the Vitalys. Detective Colon is working on behalf of her cousin Jenny; we know that now. But this guy has all the markings of a trained assassin for hire. That is the Vitaly's trademark."

"Well, what do you want to do with him?" Chasity asked.

"I'll try to scare him into giving up the info, but I don't think he'll crack. I'll just have to let him go."

Detective Samuels opened the bathroom door, and to his surprise Fox had vanished. The bathroom window was wide open.

"He escaped! Sneaky ass bastard!"

"Wow! We are dealing with professionals," Chasity responded.

"I do think you should consider moving in with me for a little while. Just until this whole thing blows over. I can protect you better if you were with me," Detective Samuels offered.

"Okay, but please don't try anything with me because I'm not in the mood."

"Cool."

She packed her things and got in her car and followed Detective Samuels to his two-bedroom condo.

"I'm impressed!" Chasity said when she entered the plush immaculate condo. "I'm not going to front. I was expecting a messy man-cave that needed three women to touch it up! But you're a very clean dude. I like that."

"One point for Tommy," he replied sarcastically.

"You don't have any kids?"

"No, I wanted some. But I was so into my career that all the women I was ever involved with couldn't withstand my career choice." He poured himself a drink. "That's why I was seeing you. I didn't have the patience for the bullshit anymore."

"I used to always say, 'What's a fine guy like you doing tricking on thots?'"

He blushed. "Thank you, you're not too bad yourself."

"What is your nationality? If you don't mind me asking."

"My mom is white and my father is African American."

"That's why you look Spanish. I always thought you were Dominican or something. I knew you were some kind of black though," she replied.

"How did you know that?" he asked curiously.

"Because you had a little swag. I can just tell."

Detective Samuels found himself ready to make a move, but he decided against it. "I'm getting tired. You can sleep in the guest room. I'll see you in the morning." He got up to go to his room.

"Wait!" Chasity grabbed his hand. "I don't want to sleep alone."

He led her to his bedroom, and they lay next to each other. Chasity snuggled up under his left armpit. "I can hear your heartbeat. It's strong." She rubbed his chest.

"Good night, Cherry."

"Good night."

Chasity pretended to go to sleep but she couldn't. There was too much on her mind.

It's not really a good night. I'm just fooling myself. People want me dead over some money. I wish it would all go away, but who am I kidding. They're not going to stop until I give them the money.

She tossed and turned.

"Baby, are you all right?" Samuels asked, noticing her inability to fall asleep.

"I'm far from all right, but I'll be okay." *As long as no hitman tries to put a bullet in my head over $1.7 million. Maybe I should leave the country.*

CHAPTER 19

Damn That Feels So Good!

"What do you mean she got away!" Rocco yelled. "What the fuck happened!" Rocco said, having one of his steroid-induced rants.

"She has a cop protecting her. He came to the door with his gun out, and he cuffed me and threw me into the bathroom," Fox reported. "He tried to scuff me up for info, but I gave him nothing."

"So you're telling me that she has her own personal security or something!" He took a swig of beer and slammed the mug down on the counter. "I don't care if she had the freaking Navy Seals protecting her! I want her and I want her now!" he fumed as he stared at Fox. "You got me?"

"I got you, boss." Fox didn't want to enrage him any more than he already was. He exited the bar.

Rocco called Jenny, and she didn't pick up the phone. "That's the fifth day in a row she hasn't picked up my calls or called me back." He threw some money on the bar and exited. He jumped in his truck and sped off headed toward Jenny's house.

******

Jenny wore her signature leopard print lingerie waiting for her new lover to appear. "Where is he? He was supposed to be here an hour ago." She kept twisting her hair and looking at her watch.

She was on to the next. Rocco didn't do it for her anymore. Especially after he went off again on one of his steroid-induced rages. There was one more incident where he exploded and punched out his own car window over a disagreement.

That wasn't the straw that broke the camel's back. One afternoon Jenny was horny so she wanted Rocco to pound her out like she stole something from him, and she needed a good sex session. Just as Rocco readied himself to enter her, Jenny's face twisted with surprise and disappointment. His penis was now half the size. *What the hell is going on! I know Rocco's dick was bigger than this!* Jenny thought as Rocco panted, trying to please her.

"Are you okay?" she asked.

"Yeah, I'm okay. I just have a lot on my mind, that's all." Rocco knew why he wasn't performing at 100%. The steroids shrunk his penis, which was a common side effect.

When Rocco was done, Jenny was left hornier than when he started. He just teased her, leaving her upset and sexually frustrated. With the violent behavior, and now a smaller penis, Jenny was sure she needed to find another lover. She was definitely finished with Rocco.

"First my wall, and then your own car window. Now your dick just shrunk to the size of a sixteen-year-old boy!

What's next? I really don't want to know," Jenny told herself after the second incident.

That's when she met Larry, or Larry Love as he liked to refer to himself. Larry wasn't like any of the other men that Jenny was with. Her heritage or her ethnicity wouldn't allow her to see a man like Larry, who was a twenty-five-year-old dark-skinned black man. At 6-feet 4-inches tall and 260 pounds of lean muscle, he was into Hip-Hop and played semi-pro football for the Giants farm team.

The two met at the local Wal-Mart shopping for groceries. They were both in the pasta aisle getting the same ingredients to make spaghetti.

"I used to buy Prego and Ragu, but now I use homemade Mama Leona's," Larry said to Jenny as she reached for the generic spaghetti sauce. "One meal with Mama Leona'a homemade sauce and you'll never go back." He smiled and Jenny's eyes lit up like fireworks.

Wow! This young man is so freaking handsome!

She often thought black men were handsome, but wouldn't take it any farther than the thought. For some reason Larry was stunning to her, his dark skin and high cheek bones with the glimmer in his eyes that only winners have. Maybe it was his innocent young charm, or the huge bulge in his sweatpants that forged the arrow that struck her heart. Whatever the case, Jenny caught an instant bout of severe *Jungle Fever*. She suddenly had an insatiable desire for chocolate.

"Hi. My name is Jenny." She smiled with a hint of seduction in her eyes. "Did anyone ever tell you that you could be a model?"

Larry was caught off-guard. "Not really, but that's a great compliment coming from a beautiful woman like you." He stuck out his hand for a formal introduction. "My name is Larry Davidson. All my friends call me Big LA or just plain LA."

"Can I just call you Larry? I'm not used to calling people by street names. No offense."

"None taken." He looked at her ring finger. Jenny had long ago taken her wedding ring off. "I see you're not married."

"I'm a widow. My husband was just buried a few days ago." Jenny bent her head in grief. "We had two boys together, now I'm a single mother raising two boys on my own."

"I'm sorry to hear that." Larry shook his head. "If you ever want a friend to talk to, here's my number." Larry handed her a business card with his name and occupation. It read: Linebacker, Giants' Farm Team. It had his number and his Facebook, Instagram, and Twitter names listed as well.

"Wow! You're a linebacker for the Giants!"

"No, for the farm team. It's the semi-pro team that some have to play with in order to get drafted to the pros."

"Oh, I see. Well, that's quite an accomplishment, Larry."

"Well, you have my number. Use it if you feel lonely."

Jenny took one last look at his crouch before he turned around. *Jesus H Christ! The size of that bulge is incredible!*

When Jenny went home, all she could think about was Larry and his bulge. She decided to visit all of his social media pages to view his pics. He posted pictures and videos of him in the gym working out with his shirt off. Those pictures sent Jenny over the edge. She got out her favorite dildo and went to her room with the laptop. She had to be quiet because the boys were still up.

She scrolled through his pictures as she let the head of the dildo play with her vagina lips. Then she saw a video where Larry's magnificent bulge was showing, and she inserted the dildo fully into her vagina.

"Yes! I want that big black dick in me right now!" She was so caught up in the moment she didn't realize VJ heard her.

"Mom!" he yelled with his ear next to the door. "Are you all right?"

She rushed to put the dildo away and waited a few seconds before she opened the door. "I'm fine. I want you and your brother to pack a little bag for a few days. You're going to your grandmother's for the week. Mommy needs a little vacation. With your father's funeral and all, I just need a break."

"Okay, I love it at Grandma's! She lets us eat whatever we want, and we get to stay up all night! Yay!" VJ ran off to tell his little brother the good news.

They packed their belongings and she drove them to the Vitaly Estate, which was a mansion situated in Dix Hills Long Island. Jenny rushed back to her house and took a shower and put on her tiger print lingerie. First she left Larry a message on Facebook.

Jenny: *Hey Larry! It was nice meeting you today.*

Larry: *Likewise*

Jenny: *Truth is, I can't stop thinking about you.*

Larry: *Oh really?*

Jenny: *Really*

With her last message she sent a selfie of her playing with her pussy.

Jenny: *If you want it, come to 126 Clayton Court in Northport, I'll be waiting.*

Twenty-five minutes later, Jenny answered the door looking like a sexy tiger in heat. "Get in here and fuck the shit out of me!" She pulled Larry into the house and shut the door.

She ripped his clothes off and went down on him. "Oh my fucking God! Your dick is so fucking huge!" She stroked it and tried to fit it in her mouth. "Damn, baby!

I've never seen anything like this in my life!" It was too big, so she licked all around his shaft and the head.

"That feels good!" Larry said. "I want that tight white pussy hole!" He lifted her off her feet and laid her on the couch. He raised her nightgown to find a nice shaven vagina waiting for him to enter. Larry took a deep breath.

"Let me lick it before I stick it, to loosen it up." Larry went down on her, sucking and licking her vagina lips.

"Damn! That feels so good! Don't stop!" Jenny screamed out.

After eating her vagina for twenty minutes, it was time. Larry mounted Jenny missionary style and put his huge member at the opening of her vagina. It was too tight, but he forced it in.

"Aww!" Jenny winced. "That shit is too big! You have to spit on it or something."

Larry spit on it and his penis was able to get in. He pumped in and out slowly until she got used to his size. Jenny moaned so loud she couldn't hear herself anymore. She was lost in ecstasy, and she didn't care who heard her.

"Faster!" she demanded.

Larry did as he was told. "Like that?"

"Oh my God! I'm going to come so big!"

As soon as she said that, Larry felt the pressure pushing him out of her vagina. It was so strong he had to pull it out. As soon as he pulled his penis out, a flood of cum squirted so hard and fast it startled Larry.

"I'm cumming!" she yelled. "Oh my God, it won't stop!"

Cum squirted out of her vagina like a broken water pipe. Her eyes closed as if she was in a trance. Her body vibrated and twitched as if having a stroke. It took two minutes for her to finish and gather her composure.

"Oh my God! I've never came so much in my entire life!" She tried to catch her breath. "I've heard of women squirting like that, but I've never experienced it myself."

"I've made a few women squirt before. But not that much." Larry shook his head. "I thought you were going to pass out the way you were cumming. I've never made a woman squirt that much before. How do you feel?"

"I feel like I just died and went to heaven!" She looked up at him. "You were amazing! I never thought sex could ever be this good until today."

I can't believe that was just a week ago, Jenny thought.

Ding! Dong!

The sound of the doorbell brought her back to the present. "That's Larry!" She excitedly jumped up to answer the door.

Jenny glanced at her reflection in the hallway mirror. She puckered her lips and blew herself a kiss. When she opened the door, her smile quickly turned into a frown. Rocco stood there with a furious expression.

"Why haven't you been returning my phone calls?" His eyes were red and his breathing was erratic.

"I've been busy this past week." She was a bit frightened by his demeanor.

"I see you have your lingerie on. Are you expecting someone?" He tried to step around her, but she got in his way.

"Rocco, right now isn't a good time. I'm on my period, and I'm just not in the mood."

"Move out of my way!" He pushed her aside. "You think I'm stupid! I know you're fucking someone else!"

"Rocco, you need to leave. I'm not in the mood for this right now."

"Not in the mood for what?" He tried to kiss her. "Not in the mood to fuck?"

"I told you I'm on my period. I have really bad cramps. I don't feel good. Can't you just respect that?"

He grabbed her by the throat. "If I find out you're seeing someone else, I'm going to kill you and whoever he is. Do you understand me?"

"Rocco, you're hurting me." Jenny spoke low because he was squeezing her windpipe.

"Hey!" Larry yelled from the doorway. "Get your fucking hands off of her!"

Larry rushed him and punched him in the back of his head before he could turn around. Rocco absorbed the blow as if it were an attempt to tickle him. The steroids greatly increased his tolerance for pain. He went into overdrive with rage. Rocco turned and glared at Larry.

"So this is the guy you're fucking?" He pointed at Larry. "Didn't know you like dark meat."

Larry punched Rocco again, this time on his jaw. The blow landed right on the button of his jaw, which buckled his knees and Rocco fell to the side.

Larry didn't stop there. He pounced on Rocco and hit him in his face with all his might. Steroids or not, no human man could withstand the mighty blows that Larry hit Rocco with. Each blow opened up a new cut on his face. Larry beat Rocco in and out of consciousness with each blow.

"That's enough, Larry!" Jenny yelled. "You're going to kill him!"

Her words stopped Larry from hitting Rocco, whose face was a pulverized mess. Larry had been beaten him to a pulp.

"Is he alive?" Jenny asked. "He's not moving. Is he breathing?"

Larry bent his head down to see if he was breathing. "He's not dead, just unconscious."

"What are we going to do with him?" she asked in a panicked tone. "His family is connected with the Mafia." Her beautiful eyes filled with worry.

"I'll put him in his truck and drive him to McDonald's around the block. Just follow me and bring me back here."

"Okay, sounds like a plan."

Larry picked Rocco up and carried him on his back to his truck. He put him in the passenger side and drove him to a McDonald's parking lot and left him there. Jenny drove him back to her place.

"That was a close call." Jenny took a deep breath. "I hope he doesn't come back over here with a mob to kill you."

"I hope so too, but when he wakes up he'll remember that ass whipping. I hope he doesn't remember who gave it to him."

******

Where am I? Rocco asked himself.

"Sir, are you all right?" an officer asked.

Rocco didn't answer.

"What is your name, sir?" the officer asked again.

Rocco nodded. "I don't know . . ."

"Sir, we need to know your name."

Rocco looked at the officer and EMT worker as if they were speaking French. "I don't know what my name is."

The officer let the paramedics put him in the ambulance. While inside, the paramedic went into Rocco's pocket to see if he had any identification and found his driver's license. He passed it to the officer.

"Rocco Vitaly," the officer said out loud. "If this is the Vitaly that I know of, there's going to be repercussions."

"Can you tell us what happened to you?" the paramedic asked.

Rocco tried hard to remember, but there was a blank, "I, I, don't remember."

Use

"We're taking him down to South Side Hospital to be looked at. I've seen cases like this where someone was hit in the head so hard that they catch temporary amnesia. His memory will come back. It may take a week or a year, but it'll come back."

*****

Detective Colon pulled up to the scene. She heard the location over her scanner and knew it was two blocks from Jenny's house, so she headed in that direction. When she arrived at the scene and saw Rocco, she knew it had something to do with Jenny. *There's no way Rocco is this close to Jenny's house, and she doesn't know anything about this.*

"What happened here?" Detective Colon asked the police officer after flashing him her badge.

"We got a call about some guy bleeding from his face sitting in a car. When we got here, he was awake, but he couldn't tell us what happened, or his name. He must've got beaten so hard he lost his memory."

"I know who he is. That's Rocco Vitaly. He's practically family," Detective Colon replied.

"Oh really?" He paused. "Well, I hope he remembers who did this to him."

"Me too." Detective Colon drove off headed for Jenny's house. She wanted answers and wouldn't leave her cousin's home without them.

******

"Don't worry, Jenny. It'll be okay." Larry tried to calm her down.

"You don't understand. Rocco and his family are killers! I don't want anything to happen to you."

"I'm not scared. I can protect myself."

"I know you can. It's just that they have vast resources."

"I got homies in the street that'll hold me down. We not scared of some soft Italians."

Jenny saw the reflection of Detective Colon's headlights as they entered the driveway. She went to the window to see who it was. "Oh shit! My cousin just pulled up! Hide!"

"Hide! Why don't you just introduce us?" Larry suggested, looking at Jenny curiously.

"Not yet! Please! Please just hide in the guest room until she leaves!"

Larry smirked but granted her plea. "Okay, but this is the last time I'm hiding from anyone. Or you can find another piece of dick." He knew that last statement hit her in the vagina.

"I'll tell the world about us when the time is right. For now, please just go in the guest room."

Detective Colon knocked on the door, and Larry went to the guest room but left the door slightly opened.

"Hey, *cuz*," Jenny said in a mocking tone. "What brings you here?"

"Don't give me that 'hey cuz' bullshit!"

"What happened?" Jenny always had a hard time lying to her older cousin.

"You tell me. I just saw Rocco two blocks from here at the McDonald's parking lot with his face beat to a pulp. He has amnesia. He can't remember his name or what happened to him."

Jenny just looked at her. "I have no idea what happened to Rocco."

"Yeah right! And I'm the Queen of England." She stared at Jenny. "It's no coincidence that Rocco is always coming over here to see you. Now his truck winds up two blocks from here with him in the passenger side beaten to oblivion."

"I didn't do it, and I don't know anything about it." Jenny held her cousin's gaze. "What's up with Cherry? You haven't told me anything about her in two weeks. What going on?"

"She is being protected by Detective Samuels. Word is, she's living with him so he can protect her. My hands are tied, unless I can get him away from her long enough to kidnap the bitch."

"Well, for $1.7 million in cash, you better do something."

"I'm on it, trust me," Detective Colon replied.

"I hope so, because I'm starting to think you're incapable of getting the job done."

"Don't play me! I'm doing the best I can without jeopardizing my career." Detective Colon became offended.

"I'm not playing you. I'm calling it how I see it. And I see $1.7 million going down the drain to a dirty home-wrecking whore."

"Give me another week or so, and I'll deliver her to you just as promised." Detective Colon sounded desperate.

"Getting her is the easy part. The hard part is getting her to tell us where the money is," Jenny replied.

"Once I get my hands on her, I know ways of making her talk. Trust and believe that."

"Okay." Jenny let out a fake yawn. "Well, I'm tired. I have to get up early tomorrow. So I'll talk to you tomorrow."

"Okay." Detective Colon stopped at the door and turned, seeing drops of blood on the rug. "You sure you didn't see Rocco today?"

"I'm positive."

"Okay. See you tomorrow." Detective Colon exited the house.

Jenny shut the door and took a deep breath. *She knows something; she always knows when I'm lying.*

Larry came out of the room and sat on the couch.

"I heard your whole conversation," he informed Jenny.

"Oh, you did?"

"I know Cherry. She was recently involved with two guys being murdered."

"You know her?"

"Yeah, if it's Cherry with the black 650i BMW. Me and her man Torian used to play football together."

"Well, the other man that was killed in that condo was my husband Vinny."

"Wow! That's crazy." Larry was amazed at the connection that was just made.

Jenny had a lightbulb moment. "Can you get in touch with her?"

"I don't see why not."

Jenny smiled. "You might be able to help me out with a little situation." She came closer to him. "It's not illegal, and if you're able to do what I need you to do, —you're going to be paid well for just helping me out." She kissed him and grabbed his penis. "But for now I need you to help me out with something else."

"What could that be?" he asked, following her into the bedroom.

"I sent the boys to their grandmother's for the week. So you have all week to do whatever you want to me. However you want to do it."

"Now you're talking."

Larry made love to Jenny until they fell out from exhaustion.

Jenny woke up while Larry was asleep. For a brief moment she glanced at him, then turned to look at her reflection in the mirror. She didn't like what she saw; she was changing but not for the better. This whole ordeal with Vinny and the money was taking its toll on her spirit.

What have I become?

CHAPTER 20

I Need My Medicine!

"I know you're a cop and all that, but I have to get my medicine," Chasity said to Detective Samuels.

"Your medicine?" he replied in a confused tone. "What are you taking?"

"No, silly!" Chasity let out a chuckle. "I'm talking about smoking marijuana."

"Oh, you had me worried for a minute." He sighed.

He really does care about me, Chasity thought, wearing a slight smile and taking Detective Samuels appearance in.

"I have an idea . . . Why don't we go out on a date tonight?" she suggested.

Her request surprised Detective Samuels. "You want to take me out on a date?"

"Yeah, I want to take you out to my favorite restaurant."

"I'd love that, but I have to work till seven p.m. tonight."

"No problem, I'll wait for you." She smiled. "Besides, it's the least I can do after all you've done for me."

"Don't mention it. I'm just helping out a friend." He grinned.

Detective Samuels grabbed his trench coat and headed for the door. "Looking forward to our date tonight. See you later." He exited the condo.

I'm starting to like Tommy, she thought. *But I'm afraid to open my heart.*

Chasity sat on the plush money green leather couch contemplating her next move. She knew it would be awkward for her to even consider being with him. Especially after she declared she didn't want anything to do with a relationship. Detective Samuels had proven to be her knight in shining armor so many times that it became his role in her life.

"Who can I call for bud?" Chasity asked aloud. Sincere was her connect for weed, but she vowed not to deal with him anymore. "Who can I call?"

As she was going through her contacts to find a weed dealer, she got a message in her Facebook inbox. She viewed the profile and automatically noticed the face.

"That's Torian's friend Larry! I wonder why he's contacting me." She clicked on the message.

Larry: *Cherry, this is Big LA, Torian's homeboy.*

Chasity: *The one that plays football?* Larry: *Yeah, that's me. Call my phone. My number is 631-745-9876.*

Chasity: *Okay.*

She called the number. "What's up, LA?" Chasity found it strange to hear from him because they weren't friends like that.

"What's up? I wanted to link up with you, just to see how you were doing. I know it's hard for you because of what happened."

"Uhhh . . . I appreciate you reaching out, but I'm fine. I'll be okay." Chasity still didn't know his angle for this connection.

"Me and Torian were very close. That was my dude! Most people don't know we started semi-pro together. He got kicked off the team for smoking too much marijuana. He loved him some weed." Larry broke the ice.

Chasity beamed, remembering all the nights she and Torian smoked together. "I know that's right. Me too. Matter of fact, I was just looking for a new weed connect. I'm going through withdrawals."

"Oh yeah? I got you. What were you looking for?"

"At least a half a pound."

"A half a pound, huh? Yeah, I remember when we went out on a double date and you and Torian snuck off for a while and came back to the restaurant with eyes so red and tight, neither one of y'all could barely see," Larry said.

"Yeah, and your uptight date said, 'Eww, what's that smell?'" Chasity said, and they both burst into laughter.

"Yeah, she was kind of stuck up," Larry said.

"Kind of?" Chasity countered.

"All right. She was snooty and pretentious."

"Exactly." A beat passed. "I miss my boy Torian every day."

"Me too." Chasity felt herself getting teary eyed. "Anyway, I need enough to last me a while. Think you can handle that?" Chasity knew a half pound was a lot for personal use, but she had the money.

"Yeah, I do. But let me check into it and call you back."

*****

Larry hung up the phone and looked at Jenny. "She was acting kind of skeptical at first, but I got her comfortable."

"So she wants to meet up with you?" Jenny said with anxious eyes.

"Yeah, she wants a half a pound of weed," Larry replied.

"Cool. That's all I need to get her in a secluded area," Jenny spoke too soon.

"Hold on. I thought you said it was nothing illegal?" Larry was having second thoughts. "It sounds like you want to do something to her."

"Babe, I told you it's nothing illegal. She has my money. Money that was supposed to be left to me and the boys. She has no right to it, and I need her to tell me where it is, so I can get what's mine."

Larry thought about what she'd just said. "So how do you suggest on getting it from her?"

Jenny closed her eyes. "Larry, listen." She paused. "I have to do what I have to do to get the money. Law enforcement isn't helping me with it because they said she didn't put a gun to his head and make him withdraw all that money." She faked tears. "You tell me what I'm supposed to do. I have two boys to take care of and no money in the bank. That money belongs to my children! She has no rights to it!" The tears were streaming now.

"Come here, baby." Larry held her head against his chest. "I'm here for you, Jen. I'm sorry for questioning your intentions. I know you'd never do anything to hurt me."

The tears were slowing up. "I love you. I'd never, ever, put you in harm's way." She grabbed his face in her hands. "Do you hear me?"

He gazed into her eyes before answering. "Yeah, I hear you."

"Okay, so let's just get her to a place where I can interrogate her into telling me where my husband's money is. Once she gives me my money, she can go free without a scratch on her head."

Larry was hesitant but he agreed. "I'll set up the meeting."

She rubbed his hair and kissed him. "Good boy."

CHAPTER 21

I'm not ever going to get caught slipping again!

I can't stop thinking about Tommy. I must be tripping, but he is so fucking sexy! Why didn't I see that before? His arms are so big. And that six-pack . . . and he's packing more than nine inches! That face . . . and his smile.

Chasity's right hand wandered toward her vagina as she thought about Detective Samuels. When she reached her clitoris she stopped. *No! Don't do it, Chasity!* she commanded.

She used that same hand to pick up her phone. "Let me send him a text."

Chasity: *Thinking of you :)*

"I hope I'm not playing myself," she said to herself before pressing send.

******

Detective Samuels was supervising a murder scene when his hip vibrated indicating that he had a new message. He looked at his phone and saw that he had a message from Chasity.

Chasity: *Thinking of you :)*

He smiled.

Detective Samuels: *Likewise. Can't wait for our date later.*

Chasity: *I have a surprise for you after dinner.*

Detective Samuels: *I love surprises. Can't wait!*

"Excuse me, Detective Samuels," a red-haired man wearing a lab coat said, interrupting his text session. "The victim had this in her hand." It was a key.

Detective Samuels put his phone away. "That's strange. Mark it as evidence."

"Yes sir."

Detective Samuels couldn't think about anything else but getting back to Chasity. He looked at his wristwatch. It was 4:40 p.m.

"Just an hour and twenty minutes left."

******

Chasity lay sprawled on the king-sized bed in Detective Samuel's master bedroom. She smiled at the thoughts running through her mind. *I'm going to fuck the hell out of this man tonight. I haven't wanted a man this bad since, well . . . since Torian.* She paused her thoughts on Detective Samuels to think about Torian.

Damn, Torian! We were supposed to be a couple. I loved you! Why did God have to take you away?

Her cell phone rang. It was Larry.

"What's up, LA?"

"I got that for you. Where do you want to meet?" he asked.

"Let's just meet at Timberline Park. It's usually secluded there."

"Okay, meet you there in thirty minutes."

"Okay." Chasity got up and put her coat on and headed for the door.

She stopped short. "I better pack my gun just in case." Chasity reached under the couch and grabbed her .25 automatic handgun and put it in her coat pocket. "I'm not ever going to get caught slipping again." Chasity headed for her car.

CHAPTER 22

Everyone Cool with the Plan?

Detective Colon pulled up in her black police cruiser. Larry was watching from the window when she exited the car, and he got nervous.

"You got real cops in on this!" His breathing became erratic, Larry was scared to death.

"Relax! That's my first cousin Jenny." Jenny saw him press the panic button.

"She has the same name as you?" Larry found that peculiar.

"It's the name of our great grandmother that was passed down through the family. She was like a saint, so the family keeps her alive by naming the girls after her."

"I get it."

Jenny opened the door for Detective Colon. When she entered the house, she looked at Larry as if he was a criminal.

"Who's this guy?" She snarled . "You know how I feel about bringing outsiders into our business."

"Jenny, this is Larry. Larry is the one that is luring Miss Cherry into our trap."

"Oh, okay." She eased up. "So he knows about the money?"

"He knows everything he needs to know," Jenny replied sternly. "Now, here's the plan. Larry is meeting up with Cherry to sell her a half pound of weed. When they make the transaction, me and cuz will roll up like the Feds and put the cuffs on her and take her away. Anyone watching will see that Larry didn't do anything wrong. You can just drive away like nothing happened."

Larry liked the last part of the plan where he drove away like nothing happened. "I'm just trying to keep my hands clean. All I need is to get caught up in some shit and there goes my chances in the NFL."

He's starting to sound like a pussy! Jenny thought. "Everyone cool with the plan?" Jenny asked.

"I'm cool with it," Detective Colon said.

"Like I said, as long as my hands are clean. I'm good with it," Larry chimed in.

"Okay, let's roll."

Sweating profusely, Larry walked to his car carrying a shopping bag with a half pound of 'loud' inside it. He suspected Jenny and Detective Colon should be in the unmarked cruiser and on their way.

When Larry pulled in, Chasity was already parked in a remote section. He rolled up and parked next to her BMW and waited before getting out. He knew Detective Colon and Jenny needed time to pull up on them. Timberline Park was only fifteen minutes from Jenny's house. The timing had to be right.

What the fuck is he waiting for? Chasity wondered, watching him through her windshield. She could see that Larry's shirt was drenched in sweat, so she kept her right hand on her gun inside her jacket pocket and gripped the trigger.

"Yo, you good, LA?" she asked, noticing his window was rolled down.

"I'm good." Larry's breathing pattern changed and his short breaths made his shoulders rise and fall rapidly. "I'm getting out now." He slowly exited the truck with the shopping bag in his hand and approached Chasity and handed her the bag.

She stuck her nose in the bag and inhaled. "This is exactly the shit that I wanted. That stinky!"

Larry immediately walked back to his truck without collecting the money.

"Yo, I didn't give you the money yet!" He hopped in and started up his truck and put it in reverse.

"Hey!" Chasity yelled.

A black cruiser pulled up and Detective Colon and Jenny hopped out with the quickness. "You're under arrest!" Detective Colon ordered as she pointed at Chasity.

"What the fuck! You're the same officer that tried to run me down!" Chasity pulled out her gun.

"She's got a gun!" Jenny yelled.

Detective Colon went for her service weapon, but she was too late on the draw. Chasity let off a shot right in her direction, missing Jenny by inches.

"Put down your weapon!" Chasity demanded. "I'm on to you, Detective Colon! I know all about your cousin, and I know what you want."

Detective Colon put her hands in the air, with the gun in her right hand. "If you know what we want, why don't you just give my cousin the money and walk away!"

"That money belongs to me!" Jenny rushed Chasity and threw a punch that landed right on Chasity's lips. She dropped the gun and blood erupted from her mouth. Detective Colon picked up Chasity's gun.

"You home-wrecking slut! You broke up my family! I hate you!" She tried to throw another punch but Chasity blocked it.

"All right. That's enough! Let's try talking!" Detective Colon suggested, breaking Jenny and Chasity apart.

"Look, I have two sons to raise, and Vinny left us with *nothing*! *Nothing!* I kept telling him to get a life insurance policy, but he never made it down to the lawyer's office to finalize it. It isn't fair!" she cried.

Chasity responded with a light shrug as she wiped the blood from her mouth. "I understand, but that's not my problem."

"It's not your problem!" Jenny tried to free herself from Colon's grasp to no avail. "Let me go!" She twisted and turned and flailed one arm, trying to hit Chasity. "I'ma kill this bitch! Let me . . . go!"

"Stop it! Jenny, calm down! Just talk to her and see if we can't resolve this peacefully first." Detective Colon put a tighter grip on Jenny's arm. "We all have too much to lose. I'm sure we can come to an agreement." Detective Colon looked at Chasity with serious eyes.

"Do you have children?" Jenny asked Chasity.

"No."

"Well, because of you, I now have to raise my two sons without their father. You have no idea what they're gonna have to face as they grow up. Vinny's not here to show them how to be men, or what a father does when raising his boys into men."

Chasity heard every word she said, but she didn't respond. She'd never known her father.

"So, who's going to show them the right things to do so that they'll be responsible, successful men? You?" She laughed mockingly. "Yeah, I bet you didn't think about that when you started seeing another woman's husband. You never stop to think about if they have children at home or how it will affect them if they ever found out about their father."

"Listen here. Vinny and I had an arrangement. So it is what it is."

"I'm pretty sure the arrangement involved you seeing only him. I know my husband very well. He's not gonna give up that kind of money to a nasty whore who sleeps with any man who comes along with cash. Oh!" Jenny covered his mouth. "But he did just that with you, didn't he?"

"Call me what you want but I bet you won't call me broke." Chasity kept her arms folded and tapped her foot, looking away from both women.

"Come on, you two. We're not getting anywhere here," Detective Colon said. "She has two kid's for Christ's sake."

"You didn't even love him, so I can't imagine why he'd leave you his money and not think of his sons," Jenny said.

"Love him? Apparently, neither did you, or he wouldn't have been out here looking for somebody else to satisfy him sexually. Or even for companionship."

"Look, the bottom line is: you owe me and you owe my boys. You took away our security and the money you have does not belong to you."

"That's where you're wrong because see, I've already got the money. Therefore it is mine. So if you hurt me, you won't get the money. Or even if you torture me, you still won't get the money."

There's just no getting through to this . . . this . . . whore! Jenny suddenly broke down into tears. "Do you know what it's like when your ten year old asks you for things, and you have to say no because your husband withdrew all the funds, and now his sons have to suffer? Do you even think about that?" Her voice cracked.

Detective Colon released the hold she had on her cousin.

Jenny's words played on Chasity's heartstrings. She didn't know the dynamics of her situation, but she did understand what it was like being a child that needed things because she was a child at one time. A child who had gone without the most basic needs, and that included the love of a father or a mother. Which is why Chasity ended up exactly where she was. Chasity knew those boys were innocent and they shouldn't be penalized for the fuck ups of grown-ups. Just like when Chasity's uncle molested her, yet her mother cursed her for the wrong her uncle committed against Chasity. Where was the justice in that? Where was the mother who was supposed to comfort her daughter and fight for her?

Chasity's conscience battled against the selfish part within her. *I earned that money. It's mine! Vinny never said share any of it with anybody. It's not my fault Vinny left them with nothing.*

"This not just about me and my marriage that Vinny and I both destroyed. This isn't even about you. This is about two kids who've lost their father, a father who is no longer here to provide for them."

She looked at Jenny's face, and it showed a woman exhausted. Chasity remembered feeling that way after sleeping with several men throughout the week and occasionally wishing for a different life. "I guess when you put it like that . . ."

Jenny wiped her tears away. Chasity dropped her arms at her side and stopped the tears that tried to well up in her own eyes.

"All you had to do was talk to me like you're doing now. We could've resolved this."

"So what're you going to do?" Detective Colon asked, releasing a hopeful sigh. "All this back and forth is annoying. Are you going to give back the money?"

Chasity thought carefully. *Well, she does have two children by him. It's only right that I share the money with them.*

"Okay, I'll give you *some* of the money back. Not all of it."

"What the fuck you mean *some*? I need all of that money! It's mine!" Jenny yelled. "I have a mortgage, a car note, utilities, school fees, you name it."

"Look. I don't have to give you *any* of it! Beggars can't be choosers! Either take what I'm giving, or kick rocks!" Chasity turned her head to the side and squinted.

"Just take whatever she gives you, Jenny! Damn!" Detective Colon yelled. "This shit is getting out of hand. Let's just agree on an amount and call it a fucking day already!"

"How much are you willing to give me?" Jenny asked, feeling desperate.

"There's only $1.7 million. I'll give you . . ." She paused.

How much should I give this bitch? I had to suck a lot of dick to get that money. But she's right. She has to take care of his kids. "Okay, fair is fair. I'll give you half the money. Which is $850,000."

"Okay! $850,000 it is," Jenny replied.

"What about my cut?" Colon's tone of voice displayed her dismay. "You think I was chasing her around for nothing?" Colon's eyes got red as she glared at Jenny.

"I got you. You deserve at least $100,000. Is that cool?"

"At least $200,000 and I'm good." Colon rubbed her hands together in anticipation of getting what she asked for.

"Can you give up an extra $100,000 and we can call it a day, please."

"Hell no! I got $50,000 and that's all the extra I'm giving up," Chasity replied. "Can we call it a truce?"

Jenny looked at Detective Colon. "Yeah, we can call it a truce. I would've done what you did as well if I were in your shoes. Men are assholes!" She returned Chasity's gun as a measure of good faith.

Chasity led them to the storage unit where the money was located. It took them almost two hours to divide all the money. Jenny put her and Detective Colon's money in a huge duffle bag that Detective Colon had in her trunk. Chasity left her half in the unit.

"Well, that's it, $900,000 for you and $800,000 for me," Chasity said while locking up the storage unit.

"Thank you, Cherry," Jenny said in a sincere tone. "Because you didn't have to give me anything. The simple fact that you gave me half shows that you have a good heart." She hugged Chasity, grateful that she could now take care of her boys and her household.

"I thought about what you said, and you're right." Chasity looked into Jenny's eyes. "I never meant to hurt you. I'm so sorry for what happened. I never wanted any of this. My lifestyle—"

"All's well that ends well," Jenny replied.

"I know right," Chasity said. "I have to go get ready for my date tonight."

*****

Detective Colon put the duffle bag in the trunk and drove to Jenny's house. When she pulled up, Larry was already in the driveway.

"What's the deal with you and this Larry character?" Detective Colon asked, but already knew what it was.

Jenny was hesitant. "He's my new man, and I don't care what anyone thinks. He treats me like a queen, and he satisfies my every sexual need."

"Well, it's not me you have to worry about. You know how Vinny's family is about blacks. They hate them, and they are sure to disown you once they find out."

"You know what, cuz? I don't give a fuck what they think anymore." Jenny smiled and shook her head. "Their son was fucking with a black woman. Hell, he gave her all his money! So I don't care what anyone thinks, as long as he makes me happy."

"At the end of the day, that's all that matters. That you're happy," Detective Colon confirmed.

Jenny got out the car to greet Larry. "Hey baby." She wrapped her arms around his waist. "Thank you for helping me out."

"Don't worry about it," he replied.

Detective Colon opened the trunk. "Do me a favor, big man."

"What's that?"

"Carry this bag into your girl's house," she said sarcastically.

"No problem." Larry lifted the heavy bag of money and took it in the house.

"I'm so glad this ended the way it did," Jenny said.

"Me too, because things could've gotten very ugly. We could've killed one another over this money." Detective Colon looked up to the sky. "Vinny is probably happy that it ended this way too."

"Most likely." Jenny closed her eyes and opened them before speaking. "You know something?"

"What's that, little cuz?"

"I'm lucky to have family like you," Jenny said with a smile.

"Me too," Detective Colon agreed.

"I'm going to go inside and entertain my company. I'll see you tomorrow." Jenny hugged Detective Colon. "Thanks again, big cuz." She walked into the house.

Detective Colon smiled as she drove off.

*****

"So, you got your money, huh?" Larry asked when she entered the house.

"I got half of it."

"Better than nothing," he replied.

"What's better than money is that I got you."

"Oh really." Larry picked her up in his arms and carried her to the bedroom. "You know what time it is."

"No, what time is it?"

"It's love making time."

He shut the door.

CHAPTER 23

Let Me Be Real!

Chasity was able to make it back to Detective Samuels' condo, shower and get dressed ten minutes before he walked in.

"Hi, baby!" Chasity greeted him at the door with a huge hug and a kiss.

"Wow!" He was thrown aback. "What was that for?"

"I don't know. I just miss you." Chasity paused and looked into his eyes for clarity. "Let me be real. I . . . well . . . I like you a lot, Tommy."

"You do?" He couldn't believe it. "Are you okay? I mean, what brought on this change of heart?" He was scratching his head trying to figure out her angle.

"I know what I said when you first offered me the safety of your home. As we spent time together, I saw that you really cared about me. Not my pussy, or how good I can give head. You showed me genuine, sincere love." A lump formed in her throat as she spoke. "No man has ever shown me that kind of love without wanting sex in exchange. You're different, because you slept next to me and you didn't try anything. That's what I needed, companionship, and not sex for once." *Girl, you better not cry!* she thought.

"This is all new to me. I mean, I'm really caught off guard." He looked away, then back at Chasity. "I have strong feelings for you as well. We've been spending a lot of one on one time together lately. We laugh, we loved and we cried in this past week. I just didn't want to put myself out there if you didn't feel the same way."

"I'm just tired." The tears broke the dam and fell down her face. "This incident with Vinny and Torian has given me time to think about my life and where it's going. I'm tired of being a thot! I don't want to be disrespected anymore. I want a man to love me. To cherish me, to care about me. Ever since I was a little girl, men have taken advantage of me. If it wasn't my own uncle, it was guys from my neighborhood. All I ever wanted was to be loved, that's all. I mistook lust for love, and that's why I let men take advantage of me. Men that just wanted sex because that's how I put myself out there. I know I'm worth more than that. There's one man that showed me that he cares about my safety, and that man is you." She kissed his lips.

"I'm at a loss for words." He licked his lips and closed his eyes. "I don't want to mess this up."

"Shh, don't say anything. Just kiss me."

Detective Samuels slowly kissed Chasity, taking his time with every touch. He savored every moment, as did Chasity. They were locked in a lover's embrace that neither one wanted to disengage from. They didn't rip one another's clothes off like the savages they once were. This time it was different. There was a connection, an understanding. They both felt the pure intense warmth of love in its infant stage. They touched and explored, they licked and teased; the foreplay became more exciting than any time they engaged sexually in the past. There was no denying the passion. They were both ready to explode after an hour. And there was no penetration.

They lay on the bed looking into each other's eyes. Searching and finding the soul that peeps through the window of the eyes. A glimpse is all one needs to become attached on a spiritual level. This was deeper than either one of them could fathom. This was the opposite of *'Falling in Love,'* this was *'Ascending in Love.'* Because they both were at the base level of being in love with someone. This was the first time Chasity and Tommy had experienced this type of union.

"Before we make love, I want you to know something," Chasity said in a sincere tone.

"What is it, baby?"

"I told myself that the next man I have sex with, is the last man I'm having sex with. Or at least for as long as you'll have me in your life. Are you ready for that type of commitment? If not, we don't have to waste each other's time and energy."

"I can see myself with you. I think I'm falling in love with you," he replied. "I am in love with you."

He entered her, and they both gasped as if receiving a rush of oxygen from a high altitude. The emotions were so intense they became suspended in time and space. Nothing else mattered in the universe but their bond, their newfound connection to love. Each moment was marked with immeasurable bliss. They were both synced to a rhythm slowly building into a grand crescendo. They came at exactly the same time, creating an eruption of sensation so massive it felt like infinity, but it was only minutes.

"Wow! That was incredible!" Chasity said, gasping for air. "I never knew love could ever feel like this."

"I've never made love before today," he replied, putting his confession into the universe and before the woman he trusted. "I know this to be a fact."

"Neither have I. I was just having sex, because this was something totally different!"

"I know one thing. I'm hungry as hell. But I don't want to move," Detective Samuels declared.

Chasity smiled. "Let me order some Chinese food for us." She grabbed her cell phone. "I have a text message from Larry."

Larry: ***Sorry to bother you but Torian's funeral is tomorrow at Pinelawn cemetery. Just wanted to know if you were going.***

I should go to pay my final respects to the man I loved. I know his wife doesn't want me there, but I feel the need to see him one last time, Chasity thought.

Chasity: *OK that's cool. See you there.*

"Who was that, baby? If you don't mind me asking," Detective Samuels asked.

"I don't mind you asking me anything." She kissed his forehead. "That was Torian's friend Larry. He was asking if I was attending Torian's funeral tomorrow."

"Are you going?"

"I wasn't at first, but something is telling me to just go to say good-bye." Chasity's eyes swelled up with tears but she didn't cry. She held them back.

"Now order that food. That lovemaking got me famished for some reason," Detective Samuels said.

"Me too. I guess that's one of the side effects of making real love," Chasity said.

"I guess so because I've never felt this hungry after having sex."

They ordered their food and ate. Afterward, they made more love. This time they didn't stop for two hours. Exhausted, they both fell into a deep sleep. During the course of Chasity's deepest dream state, Torian made his grand entrance once more.

Yellow daisies filled the field, and the huge oak tree stood in its usual spot, in the middle of the field. Unlike the previous dreams in which Chasity wore all white, this time she was dressed in all black as if attending a funeral. She searched for Torian by the tree where he normally appeared in previous dreams.

"Torian!" Chasity yelled. "Where are you?"

She searched for him, then suddenly he appeared behind her. He tapped her on the shoulder and she turned. His presence startled her.

"Torian! You scared me. Why were you hiding from me?" she asked.

"The tree is a symbol of our true connection," Torian said.

"I don't get it. What do you mean this tree is a symbol of our true connection?" She looked confused.

"This tree is a symbol of our true connection."

"How? Please tell me what you mean, Torian." She panted

"The tree." He looked toward the tree. When Chasity looked at the tree and turned back to Torian, he disappeared.

"Torian! Torian! Torian!"

"Baby, wake up!" Samuels shook Chasity until she awoke from her bad dream, "You were having a nightmare."

She rose from her position. "I know. It's the same one I've been having since the incident."

"You were shouting, *'Torian!'* and *'The tree!'*"

"That's what my dreams have been consistently about. Torian standing by a huge oak tree in a field of yellow daisies or red roses. I guess the roses represent the love we shared, I'm not sure about the daisies though." She was visibly shaken.

"It's okay." He held her and kissed her. "It's only a dream, baby. I'm here."

She felt comforted by his words and his touch and she was able to relax. Chasity looked at the clock on the wall. It was 6:30 a.m. *I can rest for two and a half more hours,* she thought as she nestled up in Samuel's arms.

With Tommy, she felt a certain security that allowed her to rest assured. Something she'd never experienced before when being with a man.

"I feel so complete and safe lying with you," she whispered.

"That's because you are safe," Tommy said.

Chasity closed her eyes and smiled while rubbing his chest. "I'm so lucky."

"Not as lucky as I am."

Her former life invaded Chasity's thoughts and Kat popped up in her mind. *She used to be my best friend. I wonder if she's still thotting out there.*

She sighed, and Detective Samuels noticed she went from happy to worry in a split second.

"What's wrong? Did I miss something?" he asked.

"I was just thinking about my former partner in crime, Kat. I was wondering if she was still out there, and I got a feeling of concern because I know she's still out there. I just hope she's safe. I know all too well about the dangers of that life."

"Let's just hope that she's safe. That's all we can ask for at this point."

"You're right." She snuggled up closer and went to sleep.

******

Bay Shore Motor Inn

Knock! Knock!

"Who is it?" Kat asked, trying to make out the face through the dirty peephole.

"It's Bosco."

"Oh." She opened the door.

As soon as he was in the room, he took out an ounce of sour diesel marijuana. It was so smelly it stank up the whole atmosphere.

"That must be the shit because it's stinking like it!" Kat said when he pulled out the ounce.

"Yeah, this is a rare strand of sour that they only have in California."

"What do I owe you?"

Bosco looked down at her breasts and vagina. "I don't know. Let me see." He turned her body so he could see her ass. "I think I'll have a pound of that!" He smacked her on the backside.

"I thought you'd never ask." She slipped out of her shorts and dropped to her knees.

Kat did her usual tricks to make Bosco come. When she was done she noticed Bosco lingering and searching the room with his eyes. Bosco was up to something.

"I got some things to do." She motioned him to exit. "I'll talk to you later, Bosco."

"Where's the fucking money, thot?" Bosco grabbed Kat by her neck.

"I don't have no money, Bosco! Let me go!"

He smacked her to the ground. "Bitch! I know you got a couple thousands in here! Stop playing with me!"

"Okay! I'll give you the money. Just don't hurt me."

She reached under the mattress. "Here!" When her hand returned, it held a small .25 automatic handgun.

Bap! Bap!

Kat shot Bosco two times in his head. He slumped to the ground. Bosco was dead in an instant.

"See what you made me do!" Kat yelled as tears streamed down her face. "This shit is all fucked up now!"

She didn't know what to do or who to turn to. Kat just sat on the bed holding the gun and thought about putting it to her head and pulling the trigger. She knew her life was about to take a turn for the worse.

It didn't take long for the Suffolk County Police to come banging on the door. The gunshot was heard throughout the building. The hotel clerk was alerted by a cleaning lady that happened to be next door to Kat. She heard the entire ordeal.

"Suffolk County Police! Open the door!"

"Fuck!" Kat panicked. "Wait a minute. I'm coming."

She took too long so they kicked in the door.

Boom!

"Get on the floor!" the officer yelled.

Kat got on the floor with her hands behind her head.

The officer looked at Bosco's body lying face down with blood all over the carpet.

"You have the right to remain silent. Anything you say, can and will be held against you in a court of law." One officer read her rights while the other cuffed her hands behind her back.

"Get Detective Samuels down here. This is a job for homicide."

******

Chasity moved as slow as molasses getting dressed for Torian's funeral. She had butterflies in her stomach all morning. Considering the circumstances, she had every right to feel some kind of way. His friends and family would be there, and most of them wouldn't have anything nice to say to her. They all still felt like this was all her fault.

I'm not there to see anyone. I'm there to pay my respects. At the end of the day we loved each other, Chasity thought.

Samuels was in the shower while she got dressed. When he came out he quickly got dressed. "See how fast that was. Why can't women ever get dressed in a timely fashion?" he asked sarcastically.

"It takes time to prepare beauty."

His phone rang. "That's my job," he answered the phone. "What's up?"

"We have a homicide at Bay Shore Inn. All the other Homicide Detectives are out on assignments. We need you on this one."

"Dammit! I was off today!" he fumed.

"I know, but I had no choice."

"Okay, I'll be there in fifteen." He hung up the phone.

"What's the matter, baby?" Chasity asked.

"I have to go investigate a murder at Bay Shore Inn. They're short of staff today so I have to go in."

"That's where me and Kat use to hustle."

"I don't know anything yet, but I'll keep you posted. I'll see you later." He kissed her and headed for the door.

"I guess I'll have to be strong by myself. At least I'll be with Big LA and his girl."

Chasity put the finishing touches on her makeup and her outfit. She took one last look at herself before heading out the door.

"Not bad, not bad at all." She walked out the door headed for the funeral.

Why am I doing this? Something is pulling me in that direction, as if I need to go for closure of some sort, Chasity thought. She looked at her reflection in the BMW before getting in and starting it up.

I don't know what it is, but there's only one way to find out.

CHAPTER 24

This is Strange!

Detective Samuels pulled up and rushed to room 115. He wanted to get in and out, so he could be by Chasity's side at the funeral. He knew how much she needed his presence.

"What's the deal here?" Detective Samuels asked the officer in charge of the crime scene.

"We got a call about two shots going off in this room. When we got here we found this body and a female, age twenty-three by the name of Kathy 'Kat' Hendricks."

Kat! he thought. *Chasity was just talking about her.*

"Oh, and I almost forgot"—he held up the .25 automatic handgun—"We also found the murder weapon."

"This looks like an open and shut case," Detective Samuels said.

"Not quite." The officer pointed to a police cruiser with Kat sitting in the back. "This crazy dame is claiming she didn't do it. She says that she came to the room, and he was already there dead. Which I find hard to believe considering that she checked positive for gunshot residue on her hands and wrists."

"Oh, I get it. She's trying to act crazy to get an insanity plea," Detective Samuels responded.

"I guess, but it's not going to work. Word is, she was a prostitute, so she was fully aware of what she was doing."

"I'll go talk to her." He strolled over to the car, and the window was down. "Hey, Kat. How're you doing?"

"How the fuck do you think I'm doing!" she replied.

"You know we have enough evidence to indict you for murder?"

"I don't give a fuck what you got! I didn't do it! Like I said, I came in the room and he was dead already."

"If that's your story."

"And I'm sticking to it."

"Your choice, but it might make the judge slam you harder because you show no remorse."

"Listen, I don't want to talk unless it's to my lawyer!" Kat became belligerent by yelling her demands and shouting obscenities.

With that said, Detective Samuels walked away. He went back to the room and made his report. There was nothing else for him to do. The case was cut and dry. "I'm going home. I wasn't even supposed to be here today," Detective Samuels declared.

"Okay, see you tomorrow, Samuels. We got it from here."

Detective Samuels looked at his watch. "It's still early. Maybe I can catch her before the funeral is over." He jumped in his car and headed for Pinelawn Cemetery.

******

Chasity spotted Larry and Jenny sitting in his truck waiting on her to arrive. They spoke on the phone and made arrangements to walk in together. She parked the BMW and strolled over to them. They got out of the vehicle, and they all walked together into the church. There were at least a hundred people there paying their respects.

Knowing Torian's ex-wife would also be there played on Chasity's nerves. She was embarrassed about what she used to do. Which wasn't that long ago. Nevertheless, she held her head up high and ignored the whispers as she passed by.

"Ain't that the bitch that got him killed?" one man whispered loud enough for Chasity to hear. She just kept moving.

When she got to the casket, she could hardly look at Torian. She kept shaking her head back and forth. *Why?*

His ex-wife and his sons were in the front row crying. Tondra saw Chasity walking up to the casket.

"Fucking thot! What're you doing here?" she shouted.

Chasity pretended she didn't hear a word Tondra said. She kept moving with the viewing procession. She saw three people that she wouldn't have expected to be there. Especially one of the individuals.

Uncle Tony? What the fuck is he doing here? And my mother and sister? This is strange.

They were equally shocked to see her. They had heard how Torian was killed, but they never got the name of the female they were told was involved.

"What the fuck is she doing here?" Chasity's mother said to her brother Tony.

"I don't know," Tony replied. "I didn't even know she knew Tory."

"She never did get a chance to meet him because you went upstate for all that time."

"True," Tony said.

"Was that who Tory's ex-wife was shouting at a minute ago?" Chasity's mother asked.

"I don't know, but it looked like it," Tony replied.

Chasity wanted to hit Tony with something once she saw him. The memories of him molesting her ran through her mind. Mixed emotions twirled around her head like a mental tornado. Chasity hadn't seen her family since she was fourteen years old.

She had to walk past them.

"How you been, Chasity?" her mother said as she was passing. Her mom looked terrible from the years of alcohol abuse. There were bags under her eyes and wrinkles lined her brown skin like a prune.

"Great, and yourself?" Chasity was happy to see her family, but she sensed the feeling wasn't mutual.

"I'm okay." She looked her in the eyes for a brief moment, then she rolled them and turned her head.

"And you, Sara?" she said to her sister. "How have you been?"

"I'm fine." Sara was genuinely happy to see her sister considering the circumstances.

She glared at her Uncle Tony with hatred in her eyes. She couldn't bring herself to say anything to him. So she didn't. But as she looked in his face she saw something, something uncanny that disturbed her deeply. She couldn't help but notice the striking resemblance that her Uncle Tony had with Torian.

This is too strange, she thought.

"Well, how're you doing, Chasity?" Tony said, breaking the ice. "It's been a long time." He smiled and she wanted to throw up.

"It sure has," she replied with a cold tone. *I could kill you where you stand.*

"Did you know my son?" Tony asked.

"What son?" Chasity asked, confused.

"Torian, your cousin," he said.

The room started spinning.

"What did you say?" Chasity asked.

"Did you know my son, Torian? Your cousin," Tony said.

"Your son? My cousin?" Chasity couldn't fathom the words she'd just heard. "Torian is my cousin?"

"Your *first* cousin," her mother said.

"This can't be true!" Chasity ran to the bathroom. "This can't be happening!"

"What's wrong with her?" Tony asked.

"I couldn't tell you. I haven't seen that child in over ten years. Today was the first time I've seen her since she was thirteen or fourteen years old. She got to be in her early twenties. I done forgot her damn age!" her mother said.

******

Chasity sat in the bathroom stall crying and going over all the images of Torian in her mind. Then she thought about the dreams and what they really meant. Torian was trying to communicate with her in the dream. *The tree represents our true connection.*

Those were the words he spoke in the dream.

"The family tree! Now I know what you were trying to tell me." She wiped the tears. "You were trying to tell me that we're first cousins."

Sara entered the bathroom looking for Chasity.

"Cherry!" Sara yelled. "Are you in here?"

Chasity wiped the tears away before coming out of the stall. "Yeah, I'm in here."

"Is everything okay?" Sara asked.

"Yeah, I'm fine." Her voice was quivering. "I'm ready to go."

"Okay, but if you want to talk about it, I'm still your sister." Sara exited the bathroom.

I still can't believe Torian is my first cousin. I feel so disgusted! she thought.

She didn't want her family to know why she was upset. Then she would have to make up a story to tell them because she wasn't ready to embarrass herself by telling the truth. That the man she was dealing with was indeed her first cousin. She wanted to save herself the humiliation.

"I want Tommy." She exited the bathroom.

"You okay?" Larry asked.

"I'm fine. Just had stomach cramps," Chasity replied. "I'm ready to go."

"Okay, I guess I'll talk to you later," Larry replied.

"Yeah, we'll talk later." Chasity walked to her car.

As soon as she was about to pull off, Detective Samuels pulled up. She saw him so she pulled up next to him.

"I have to get out of here, baby," she said.

"Is everything okay?" he asked, noticing the anguish in her expression.

"No, everything is not okay." A flood of tears came down her face.

"What happened?"

"Can we get out of here? I don't want to talk here. Meet me at the condo."

They drove to the condo. Chasity slowly walked to the door as if she were on the green mile to her own execution. Although she didn't want to tell Samuels the devastating news, she knew she had to be honest with him. She sat on the couch holding her head in her hands. Detective Samuels came in right after her and he gave her his full attention.

"So, tell me what happened." He felt as if he had to brace himself.

Out of nervousness she rubbed her hair before speaking.

"Well, I saw my mother, my sister, and my Uncle Tony at the funeral sitting in the front row with the family."

"Okay, so what does that mean?"

"It means that Torian was my Uncle Tony's son. Which means I was fucking my first cousin."

Detective Samuels was shocked. "Are you serious!"

"Apparently, Torian is my Uncle Tony's son. I didn't know him because my uncle wasn't a family man. He has kids all over the place. He barely claimed any of them. So how was I supposed to know that Torian was my cousin?" She was mad at herself.

"Wow, this is some deep shit."

"Tell me about it!" Chasity stood. "I'm going to roll me a fat ass blunt! I need that shit right now!"

Chasity went to her stash and grabbed an ample amount and rolled it up. She went out on the balcony to smoke. Detective Samuels followed.

"Listen, I know you're feeling messed up about the situation. But it's not your fault. How were you supposed to know?" he said in a compassionate tone.

"If I wasn't such a thot, I would've waited to get to know him before I got with him!"

"That's not fair to you or him. You can't beat yourself up over this."

"You're right, it's not my fault." She took a hefty pull of the blunt, held it in and then exhaled. "But I do know what my fault is."

"And what's that?" he asked curiously.

"Dealing with a married man in the first place. When I found out Torian had a wife and two kids I should've left him alone. I'm so stupid!" She banged her fist on the balcony's railing.

"It's okay, you didn't know." He hugged her closer to his chest. "You know what?" He waited for her to respond but she didn't. "Baby, I said do you know what?"

She took another toke. "No . . . what? What's on your mind?" Chasity answered.

Detective Samuels turned the conversation in a different direction.

"I feel like I was ready for this." He kissed the top of her head.

"For what?" Chasity asked, turning toward him. "Ready for all my crazy ass mess of a life?"

"Naw. Baby, that is your past, and you're gonna have to learn to leave it there. You'll have to forgive the people that hurt you and the people that you've hurt. Do you understand me?" He looked down at her with a solemn expression.

When she gazed into his loving eyes, Chasity nodded because she'd release a flood of tears if she allowed herself to respond. She knew what he was saying was the only way she'd be able to go on with her life and true happiness. She gave permission for two tears to fall from her eyes but no more. Then she sniffed and inhaled the blunt once more.

"Baby, I meant that I feel like I am ready for you. To fully love you . . . This is the first time I've considered being in a committed relationship since my divorce. And it feels good. For once I feel like a man who's loved, and I'm ready to love. I thank God for putting you in my life! You've shown me that there is a thing called love." He smiled and gently kissed her lips.

"I love you, Tommy." She put the blunt out on the railing and pressed her face against his muscular chest and closed her eyes.

"I love you too, baby." He took a deep breath and closed his eyes before speaking again. "Can I ask you something?"

"Sure." She didn't know where he was going, but she knew it was going to be a serious question.

"Do you ever want to have kids?"

Their eyes met. "Good question. I wasn't thinking about it until now," she responded honestly. "The idea itself is scary. Because my own mother didn't protect me when I needed her to protect me most. But I want to make sure I'll always protect my child when he or she needs me to."

"And we will."

"I love you so much." Chasity squeezed his waist tight.

"So guess what?" he asked.

"What?" she asked innocently.

"I want kids, and there's only one way to make them." He kissed her briefly.

"And how's that?" she answered playfully.

"Like this!" He scooped her up in his arms and carried her to the bedroom.

Chasity and Winston made love with the intentions of making babies.

THE END!

www.ingramcontent.com/pod-product-compliance
Lightning Source LLC
Chambersburg PA
CBHW070627170726
48291CB00003B/906